Learning English From Uncle Lee 3 : A Poor Man's Will

跟李伯伯學英文 3

窮人的遺囑

A Poor Man's Will

李家同 著

康士林·鮑端磊 譯

潔子 繪

目　錄

難忘的聖誕夜
An Unforgettable Christmas Eve

康士林　譯

　　女服務生告訴我們，老太太每年聖誕夜都會來享受一頓正式的晚餐，總有一位計程車司機會去接她，飯店主人幾乎免費地供應她這一頓飯，她只象徵性地付一些錢，事後也會有一位計程車司機送她回家。

　　The waitress told us that the elderly woman each year came to enjoy a proper meal on Christmas eve. There was always a taxi driver who went to get her, and the store manager gave her the meal almost free of charge. She only had to pay a symbolic amount of money. After the meal, there was another taxi driver who would drive her home.

明天就是聖誕節了，今天晚上，在我們國家，很多年輕人會以狂歡舞會來慶祝，很多大飯店會推出聖誕大餐來招待那些有錢人。在歐美，各大百貨公司的老闆們一定都在檢討這幾天他們貨物銷售的業績。如果聖誕節百貨公司銷售的情形不理想，不僅商人們不快樂，連正要去度假的經濟部長都會沮喪，因為這會象徵經濟的不景氣。

對於虔誠的基督徒，聖誕節當然和宗教儀式有關，今晚，很多大教堂會傳出優美的聖歌，神父和牧師們會向信徒們講道。

---

celebrate (v.) 慶祝　　　　　　　well-off 富裕的
riotous (adj.) 放縱的、狂歡的　　examine (v.) 檢視
lavish (adj.) 豐富的、鋪張的　　figure (n.) 數據

Tomorrow will be Christmas; this evening, in my country, many young people will celebrate by going to riotous dancing parties. Many large hotels will prepare lavish Christmas dinners for those well-off. In Europe and the United States, the owners of large department stores will definitely be examining the sales figures for these few days. If the situation of Christmas sales at department stores is not ideal, not only will the businessmen not be happy, but even ministers of commerce will be depressed when they take their Christmas vacation, because it will augur that the economy is not healthy.

For devout Christians, Christmas of course is related to a religious celebration. This evening, many churches will pour forth beautiful hymns; priests and ministers will preach to the faithful.

---

ideal (adj.)理想的
augur (v.) 預示
healthy (adj.) 健全的

devout (adj.) 虔誠的
religious (adj.) 宗教的

　　對於絕大多數的人來講，聖誕節使我們想起閃亮的聖誕樹、聖誕卡（聖誕卡上老是畫上白雪覆蓋的大地，一些造型可愛的小屋子）、聖誕歌曲和大教堂裡莊嚴而隆重的宗教儀式。

　　我才去美國的那一年，聖誕夜我要趕到加州南部的一個親戚家去，我沒有車，不要說坐飛機了，那時，我連火車都坐不起，只好選擇了最便宜的灰狗車。大約晚上七點左右，灰狗車進入了一個不大不小的城市，乘客全體下車休息，也乘機吃晚飯。車站裡有一家飯店，雖然是聖誕夜，照常營業，也許因為這是附近唯一開張的飯店，飯店的生意很好，幾乎座無虛席。

---

sparkling (adj.) 閃亮的　　　　　　solemn (adj) 莊嚴的

For the majority of people, Christmas makes them think of sparkling Christmas trees, of Christmas cards (those "typical" ones with snow filling the earth and lovely little cottages), of Christmas carols, and of solemn religious ceremonies in church.

The first year I was in the United States, I was going to the house of a relative of mine in southern California for Christmas eve. I didn't have a car. At that time, I couldn't even afford to go by train, let alone by airplane, so I had to select an inexpensive Greyhound bus. Around seven o'clock in the evening, the Greyhound bus entered an averaged-sized city, and all the riders got off for a rest, taking the opportunity to have supper. There was a restaurant in the bus stop, which was open, even though it was Christmas eve. This probably was the only restaurant open in the neighborhood, so business was good and nearly all the tables were taken.

---

opportunity (n.) 機會   supper (n.) 晚餐

　　我們坐下以後，看到隔壁有一位老太太在吃飯，她年紀大了，手抖得厲害，喝湯的時候困難重重。外國人不可以拿起碗來喝湯，必須用湯匙將湯用手送入口中，這位老太太常因手抖而喝不到湯。有一位好心的女服務生在替很多客人服務的時候，不時抽空來幫她的忙，將湯送入老太太的口中。因為她非常忙，她所能幫的忙非常有限。

　　灰狗車中有不少年輕的乘客，大概都和我一樣屬於窮大學生的族群，有一位年輕的男孩子索性坐到老太太的旁邊去，不僅餵她喝湯，也替她切肉，整套大餐，都由他在旁邊伺候。老太太的胃口不大，大部分的菜其實

---

good-hearted (adj.) 好心的　　　　customer (n.) 顧客

After we sat down, I saw an elderly woman eating next to us who was very old and whose hands were shaking. It was only with much difficulty that she could eat the soup, for foreigners can not drink from the bowl when eating soup. They must use a soup spoon to put the soup into their mouth. This elderly woman was not able to eat the soup because of her hand shaking. There was a good-hearted waitress who, while she was waiting on many other customers, would still find time now and then to come help by putting the soup in the elderly woman's mouth. But because she was very busy, her ability to help was limited.

Many of the young passengers on the Greyhound bus were probably poor college students like myself. One young man sat next to the elderly woman and fed her the soup as well as cut up food for her. For the entire meal he sat by her side and was at her service. The elderly woman did not

limited (adj.) 受限的、有限的　　　passenger (n.) 乘客

由這個年輕人吃掉了。老太太好像沒有和年輕人說一句話，可是她不時輕輕碰年輕人的手，以表示她的感激。

女服務生告訴我們，老太太每年聖誕夜都會來享受一頓正式的晚餐，總有一位計程車司機會去接她，飯店主人幾乎免費地供應她這一頓飯，她只象徵性地付一些錢，事後也會有一位計程車司機送她回家。

老太太吃完了最後一道甜點，她莊嚴地拿了一些錢放在桌上。一位服務生替她穿上了大衣，有一位飯店的職員站在飯店門口替她開門，也向她微微地鞠躬，門

---

appetite (n.) 胃口　　　　　　appreciation (n.) 感激
occasionally (adv.) 偶爾　　　free of charge 免費

have much of an appetite, so most of the food was actually eaten by this young person. It seemed as if the elderly woman didn't say a single word to the young person, but she would occasionally touch lightly his hand to show her appreciation.

The waitress told us that the elderly woman each year came to enjoy a proper meal on Christmas eve. There was always a taxi driver who went to get her, and the store manager gave her the meal almost free of charge. She only had to pay a symbolic amount of money. After the meal, there was another taxi driver who would drive her home.

After the elderly woman had her last course, the dessert, she would solemnly place some money on the table. A waiter would help her put on her coat and another worker from the restaurant would open the door for her, and

---

symbolic (adj.) 象徵性的   course (n.) 一道菜

口一輛計程車熱了引擎以待，司機開了車門扶老太太進去。

　　有趣的是，這些服務生和飯店老闆都不是基督教徒，他們是猶太人，猶太人是不過聖誕節的，所以他們才可以在聖誕夜提供這種服務，基督徒都休假去了。

　　有一年，又是聖誕夜，我到紐約的聖派崔克大教堂去望子夜彌撒，這場彌撒是向全國電視廣播的，果真不凡，聖誕歌曲唱得十全十美，大教堂的裝飾更是美到了極點，我發現誰也不向誰打招呼，更令我難過的是：地下鐵裡到處都是無家可歸的流浪漢。

---

engine (n.) 引擎　　　　　　　extraordinary (adj.) 非凡的
observe (v.) 慶祝、過⋯⋯節日

slightly bow towards her. With the engine of the taxi already started, the driver would open the taxi door for her and help her in.

What was interesting was that these waiters and the restaurant manager were not Christians; they were Jews, who do not observe Christmas. They were the ones working on Christmas eve so that the Christian workers could have the night off.

One year, it was again Christmas eve, and I went to St. Patrick's Cathedral in New York City for Mass, which was broadcast throughout the country. It was extraordinary; the carols were sung most beautifully, and the church was decorated exquisitely. What I discovered however was that no one greeted each other. And what made me even sadder was that in the subway nearby homeless men were

---

decorate (v.) 裝飾   exquisitely (adv.) 雅致地

　　人人都過聖誕節，可是很少人會想到聖誕節真正的意義。耶穌基督降生為人，希望我們大家能夠彼此相愛，可是我們已經有了一個固定的慶祝聖誕節方式，送聖誕卡，吃聖誕大餐，上教堂，唱聖誕歌曲。可是這些行為能夠使世人感到愛與關懷嗎？這種行為是紀念耶穌基督降生最好的方式嗎？

　　我常常想起那些在加州南部小城好心的服務生，他們說：「我們不是基督徒，所以我們不過聖誕節。」可是他們卻讓那位老太太感到無限的溫暖。如果我們問那些聖誕夜上教堂的信徒們，他們一定會說：「我們是基督徒，所以我們要過聖誕節。」問題是：光靠上教堂就

everywhere.

Everyone likes to celebrate Christmas, but very few people think of the real meaning of Christmas. Jesus Christ was born for us and hopes that we will all love each other. But we already have a set way to celebrate Christmas: sending Christmas cards, eating our Christmas dinner, going to church, and singing Christmas carols. But are these actions able to make people of the world feel love and concern? Are these the best way to remember the birth of Jesus Christ?

I often think of those waitresses and waiters in the little city in southern California. They said, "We are not Christians, so we do not celebrate Christmas." But they allowed that elderly woman to experience unlimited warmth. If we could ask the faithful who go to church on Christmas eve why they do, they would definitely say, "We are Christians so we want to celebrate Christmas." But the

experience (v.)體驗、感受　　　unlimited (adj.) 不受限的

算過一個有意義的聖誕節嗎？

也許，那些猶太人，當他們招待那位老太太的時候，才在過一個耶穌基督所喜愛的聖誕節。

——原載一九九八年十二月二十四日《聯合報》

question is, is it meaningful enough to celebrate Christmas by just going to church?

It might be that those Jews, when they took care of that elderly lady, were really celebrating the Christmas loved by Jesus.

懼童症
Fear of Children

鮑端磊　譯

感謝上蒼我終於得到了心靈上的平安，四十多年來，我一直生活在恐懼之中。對絕大多數人而言，中日戰爭早就結束了。對我而言，這場戰爭，直到兩年前才結束。

Thank the skies above that I have finally found peace of mind. For over forty years, I lived in the grip of abject terror. For the great majority of people, the Sino-Japanese War ended long ago. As far as I am concerned, however, that war raged on until just the last two years.

在我們這一行，日本東北大學的木村教授應該是亞洲最有名的一位，他不僅在亞洲有名，就以全世界而言，他的研究成果也是數一數二的。

　　可是木村教授好像也是一個怪人，他極少露面，從來不出國，甚至不到日本其他的地方去。有一次，我碰到一位美國教授，他曾經去東北大學客座一年，當然也常見到木村教授，他說木村教授一直獨身，不到任何同事家去作客，不參加任何家庭式的聚會，而且他似乎有些憂鬱症，常常一人發呆。

---

area (n.) 領域
academic specialization (n.) 學術專業
professor (n.) 大學教授
celebrated (adj.) 知名、頗受好評

achievement (n.) 成就
research (n.) 學術研究
odd (adj.) 奇怪的、古怪的
rarely (adv.) 極少、鮮少
travel (v.) 旅行

In our area of academic specialization, Professor Kimura of Tohoku University in Japan is a standout. He is not only celebrated throughout all Asia. The achievements of his research are among the best in the world.

Yet Professor Kimura seems to be a bit odd. He rarely shows his face anywhere, has never traveled abroad, and hasn't even seen all that much of Japan. One time I met an American professor who once spent a year at Tohoku University as a visiting scholar. He of course had often seen Professor Kimura. He said Professor Kimura was a loner. He was never a guest in the homes of his colleagues, never attended any type of family related gatherings. He seemed to suffer from depression. People would often find him staring off into the distance with a blank look on his face.

---

abroad (adv.) 往國外、在國外
visiting scholar (n.)訪問學者
loner (n.) 獨來獨往的人
guest (n.) 客人
colleague (n.) 同事

attend (v) 出席、參加
related (adj.) 相關的
gathering (n.) 聚會
suffer (v.) 為……所苦
depression (n.) 憂鬱、沮喪

　　大家總以為他發呆的時候在做研究，但是和他熟了以後，又發現他在想研究上困難問題的時候，表情其實很輕鬆；反而他發呆的時候，表情不僅嚴肅，而且常帶有些傷感的意味。

　　五年前，我去東北大學參加一個學術會議，晚宴的時候，赫然發現隔座居然是木村教授。他果真是一位內向而且表情常帶憂鬱的人，他是我們十分尊敬的長者，由於他不大說話，我們這一桌誰也弄不出什麼話題，只有悶著頭吃飯。

steeped (adj.) 埋首其中
contemplate (v.) 凝思
expression (n.) 表情
relaxed (adj.) 放鬆的
merely (adv.) 僅是、只是

severe (adj.) 嚴峻、嚴厲
wounded (adj.) 受傷的
banquet (n.) 宴會
discover (v.) 發現、覺察

Everyone usually thought that blank look on his face meant he was steeped in thoughts related to his research. But after getting to know him, you found that when he contemplated problems related to his work, the expression on his face actually looked very relaxed. As a matter of fact, when he did get that starry look, the expression wasn't merely severe. He wore the look of a badly wounded man.

Five years ago, it just so happened that I went to Tohoku University for an academic conference. At the evening banquet, I discovered that sitting beside me was none other than Professor Kimura himself. He truly was the quintessential introvert, a man with the look of depression sketched all over his face. He was an older gentleman eminently worthy of our respect. He said very little, however, and no one at our table could hit upon a topic

---

none other than 正是
quintessential (adj.) 本質上、典型的
introvert (n.) 內向的人

sketch (v.) 寫生；刻畫
eminently (adv.) 非常地
worthy of 值得
respect (n.) 尊敬

　　木村教授隔壁是一位英國教授，他為了找話題，問
我有沒有小孩，我一時興起，從皮夾裡拿了一張我女兒
的照片，她當時十歲，好漂亮的女孩子，我先遞給木村
教授，請他遞給那位英國佬。

　　沒有想到木村教授拿到照片以後，忽然手抖了起
來，照片掉到了桌上；他臉色蒼白，幾乎呼吸都有困
難，還好我們那一桌有一位東北大學的教授，他敏捷地
走過來，將正要倒地的木村教授扶了起來，扶著他走了
出去。

---

of common interest 讓每個人都
感興趣的
wallet (n.) 錢包

request (v.) 要求
expect (v.) 預期、料想
tremble (v.) 顫抖

that might be of common interest. No one had any choice but to eat quietly.

Next to Professor Kimura was a professor from Great Britain. Searching for something to talk about, he asked if I had any children. Excited, I immediately reached for my wallet and pulled out a photograph of my daughter. She was ten years old then, a lovely little girl. First I handed that photo to Professor Kimura, and then requested that he pass it onto the English fellow.

I'd never have expected it, but Professor Kimura took one glance at that picture and suddenly his hands began to tremble, and the picture fell onto the table. His face turned pale, he grew short of breath, and seemed about to fall out of his chair. Fortunately, a professor from Tohoku

---

pale (adj.) 蒼白的
short of breath 呼吸急促、喘不
過氣

fortunately (adv.) 幸運地

　　這個騷動引起了全場的注意，東北大學資訊系的系
主任也過來了，他問了怎麼一回事以後，告訴我們一件
驚人的怪事。他說木村教授有一個古怪的傾向，他害怕
看到小孩子，他之所以深居簡出，就是這個原因。因為
他學問特別好，東北大學特別讓他住在校內。東北大學
不是那種大樹成蔭的地方，週末也很少有小孩子進來遊
玩，於是木村教授就感到非常安全。

　　我當然不知道這個禁忌，當我給他我女兒的照片的

---

nimbly (adv.) 靈敏地、敏捷地
escort (v.) 伴隨、護送
disturbance (n.) 紛擾、騷動
attract (v.) 吸引、招來

attention (n.) 注意、關注
shocking (adj.) 令人震驚的
proclivity (n.) 傾向、脾性
terrify (v.) 驚嚇、使……害怕

University was at the table. Nimbly he stepped over, helped Professor Kimura to rise, and escorted him out of the room.

The disturbance attracted the attention of everyone there. The Chair of the Department of Information Science at Tohoku University also came over. After he asked what had happened, he told us something strange and shocking. He said that Professor Kimura had for many years a very odd proclivity. The sight of children terrified him. His scholarly achievements being so remarkable, Tohoku University allowed him to live on campus. The university was not a place with pockets of trees that offered shade, and so children seldom came to the campus to play on weekends. Professor Kimura therefore felt quite safe there.

I of course knew nothing of this taboo. When I gave him

---

remarkable（adj.）出色、值得關
注
allow（v.）允許
pocket（n.）孤立的一小塊區域

offer（v.）提供
seldom（adv.）很少、不常
campus（n.）校園
taboo（n.）禁忌

時候，他看得一清二楚，一個可愛中國小女孩的照片，他就崩潰了。

為什麼木村教授怕小孩子？這是個謎，可是木村教授絕對是個好人，也沒有任何反社會的行為，大家習慣了他這種怪行為，誰也不敢帶孩子去看他，也不會邀請他去家裡坐。

事後，木村教授親筆寫信給我，向我表示歉意，希望我原諒他的失禮。

木村教授當時已快到退休的年紀，這件事情以後我們就不再聽到木村教授的消息。兩年以後，他的弟子們出了一本論文集，來紀念木村教授一生的學術成就，我

---

conundrum (n.) 謎題　　　　　　express (v.) 表示、表達
accustomed (adj.) 習慣於　　　　apology (n.) 歉意
invite (v.) 邀請　　　　　　　　breach (v.) 破壞、違背

my daughter's picture, he took one look at it, a photo of a cute little Chinese girl, and just fell to pieces.

Why did Professor Kimura fear children? It was quite a conundrum. He was however clearly a good man. He had never done a thing against society. Everyone seemed to have grown accustomed to this odd behavior. People did not dare bring a child to visit him, or invite him to their home as a guest.

Afterwards, Professor Kimura wrote me a personal letter. He expressed apologies and hoped I would forgive his breach of etiquette.

Professor Kimura was at that time quickly approaching retirement age. After all this, we heard no more of him. A couple years later, his students published a Festschrift to

---

etiquette (n.) 禮節
approach (v.) 接近

retirement (n.) 退休
Festschrift (n.) 紀念論文集

也拿到了一本。

　　我一直沒有打開這本書來看，因為那幾篇論文並不是我有興趣的，去年我將書打開來看，發現裡面有好多照片，令我大吃一驚的是一張木村教授的照片，他和一大堆小孩子的合照。那些小鬼圍繞著他，一副頑皮的表情，木村教授也顯得很快樂。

　　我立刻送了一個電子郵件給我在東北大學的朋友，問他為什麼木村教授不怕小孩子了？他說他也不知道，只知道木村教授在那一次事件以後，決定去看心理學

---

flip (v.) 很快地翻　　　　　　flock (n.) 群
astonish (v.) 使……訝異　　　obviously (adv.) 明顯地

honor his lifelong academic achievements. I too got myself a copy.

I never opened that text, because the articles there just weren't my academic interest. Last year I flipped open its pages for a look and discovered a great number of photographs inside. What astonished me to no end was a picture of Professor Kimura standing there with a whole flock of children. What an expression he had on his face with those little tykes all around him. Obviously, he was very happy indeed.

I immediately dashed off an e-mail to my friend over at Tohoku University, and asked why Professor Kimura was no longer afraid of children. He said he did not know. All he knew was that after that incident (with the picture of my daughter), Professor Kimura decided to consult

---

immediately (adv.) 馬上、立刻
dash (v.) 匆匆完成

incident (n.) 事件
consult (v.) 諮詢、求診

家，顯然這位心理學家很有本領，居然將他的懼童症醫好了。

　　木村教授是位名人，對他好奇的人多得不得了。大家都想知道的：為什麼木村教授這樣害怕小孩子？

　　答案終於來了。前些日子，我收到木村教授的文章，文章裡詳細地解釋他的病因。文章用電子郵件寄來，顯然是寄給世界上相當多的人。文章很長，英文寫的，我將其中最重要的部分簡述如下：

psychiatrist (n.) 心裡醫師　　　numerous (adj.) 為數眾多
succeed (v.) 成功　　　　　　　curious (adj.) 好奇的
phobia (n.) 恐懼、恐懼症

a psychiatrist. That psychiatrist was so good that he succeeded in curing him of his phobia of children.

Since Professor Kimura was a very famous person, numerous people were very curious. The thing everybody wanted to know was this: why in the world did he once have that fear of children?

The answer finally came. The other day, I received Professor Kimura's manuscript. The words arrived by e-mail attachment, so the copies were apparently sent to a great many people all over the world. It was quite long, and all in English. What follows below are the most important points.

---

receive (v.) 接收、收到
manuscript (n.) 原稿、手稿

attachment (n.) 附件、附檔
apparently (adv.) 顯然

我的懼童症　木村太郎

　　我一直是正常的人。中日戰爭開始的時候，我在大學念一年級，可是徵兵徵到了我。最不幸的是：我被派到了中國大陸，而且我也參加了南京大屠殺。

　　請大家不要問我怎麼會做這種事的，當時我們都在絕對權威之下做的。文化大革命的時候很多年輕人參加了紅衛兵鬥爭他們的老師，事後也會後悔的，可是當時，他們大概也不會感到在做錯事吧。

---

completely (adv.) 全然　　　　draft (v.) 徵召
recruiter (n.) 招募人員　　　　absolute (adj.) 絕對的

My Fear of Children by Kimura

At one time in my life I was completely normal. When the Sino-Japanese War broke out, I was a freshman in a university. Recruiters for the military found me and I got drafted into the army. The most awful thing was that I was sent to the China mainland. In fact, I took part in the Nanjing massacre.

Please don't anyone ask me how I could have done this kind of thing. At the time everything we did was under the absolute command of our superiors. During the Great Cultural Revolution, many young people, led by the Red Guards, took part in struggles against their teachers. Later they regretted what they did. But at the time, they probably saw no wrong in what their actions.

---

command (n.) 命令
superior (n.) 長官、上司

struggle (n.) 鬥爭
regret (v.) 後悔

被殺的中國老百姓裡面，有一個小女孩，大概只有三、四歲，她看到了我，不知道是什麼原因，忽然抱住了我的腳，求我不要殺她，我當時仍然殺掉了她，而且也記得她臨死前恐怖的表情。這個表情是我一輩子忘不了的。

在戰爭期間，我們日本兵每天生活在恐怖之中，正規戰爭已經夠可怕，游擊隊的突擊更可怕，因為我們要隨時提高警惕，我反而沒有常常想到我在南京大屠殺中的罪行。戰爭結束以後，我的噩夢才開始了。

我回到日本以後，只要一看到小孩，就會想到那一

---

beg (v.) 懇求　　　　　　　　horrible (adj.) 恐怖的
in the midst of 在……　　　　attack (n.) 攻擊

Among the Chinese that got killed at Nanjing was a little girl. She was probably three or four years old. She looked at me, and I don't know why, but she hugged my feet. She begged *me not to kill her, but I went ahead and killed her anyway. What's more, I still remember the fear in her face just seconds before she died. That is a face I will never be able to forget my whole life long.*

As the war went on, we Japanese soldiers lived every day in the midst of pure terror. The war itself was horrible enough. Attacks by the guerrillas *were even more* frightening, *for we had to be on absolute alert every minute. So I at the time just never gave much thought to my crimes at Nanjing, the massacre and so on. After the war ended, my nightmares began.*

After I returned to Japan, the mere sight of a child

---

guerrilla (n.)游擊隊   frightening (adj.) 讓人害怕

個小女孩恐怖的表情，我常夢到她來報仇。慢慢地，我開始對小孩子害怕起來，總以為他們是來報仇的。

有一次，我坐在公園的一張長椅上，一顆球滾到了我腳邊，一個小男孩傻呼呼地向我跑來撿那顆球，我忽然緊張起來了，當時如果我有一把槍或一把刀，我會立刻殺掉他。

我知道我的問題非常嚴重，所以我搬進了東北大學。我不敢看電視，不敢看電影，和家人斷絕了來往，和朋友也絕了社交上的往來，至於出去旅行，我更加不敢了。我知道我該去看心理醫生的，可是我不敢，我不敢承認我的可怕罪行。

---

remind (v.) 提醒、使……回想起　　　revenge (n.) 復仇

reminded me of that little girl's expression of fear. I kept dreaming of her taking revenge on me. Gradually, a great fear of children began to arise in me. It always seemed they were seeking revenge.

One time I was sitting on a park bench when a ball rolled up against my foot. A little boy innocently ran up and grabbed it. All of a sudden a flash of anxiety overcame me. At that moment, if I had a gun or a knife, I'd have killed him right on the spot.

I knew my problem was really serious, so I moved to Tohoku University. I didn't dare look at a television, didn't dare go to movies. I cut all ties with my family. I also stopped interacting with friends. As for any type of travel, that was the last thing I could bring myself to do. I knew I should have gone to a psychiatrist, but I didn't dare do

---

innocently (adv.) 天真地、純潔地　　interact (v.) 互動

那一天，我看到了來自台灣李教授女兒的照片，我差一點兒嚇得昏倒過去。第二天，我決定去看心理醫生。長話短說，心理醫生給了我一個震撼教育，他親自陪我去一所公園。公園裡永遠都是有小孩子，他強迫我坐在那裡，有人陪著我，我對孩子的恐懼心當然小一點兒。慢慢地，我發現小孩子沒有一點兒可怕，他們從來沒有要來攻擊我，而且他們還非常可愛。

我的心理醫生幫我在附近找到了一個義工的工作，

admit (v.) 承認
accompany (v.) 陪伴
subside (v.) 減退、消失
process (n.) 過程

that either. I lacked the courage to admit my terrible crimes.

Then one day, I saw a picture that belonged to Professor Lee, who came from Taiwan. The picture was of his daughter. I was so frightened that I almost passed out. The next day I decided to consult a psychiatrist. To make a long story short, the psychiatrist gave me a shocking lesson. He himself accompanied me to a public park. Little children were constantly in that park, and he forced me to sit there. With someone else by my side, naturally my fear of children began to subside. It was a very slow process. By and by, I discovered children were not scary at all. They had no desire to hurt me. The fact is that they were very cute.

My doctor helped me to find volunteer work in that

---

by and by 很快、不久　　　　　volunteer (adj.) 自願的

替一班三年級的小學生做課外算術的溫習，小孩子一個一個地來找我，由我出習題給他做。一開始有一位心理醫生的助理在旁邊看我，後來沒有了。不瞞你們，孩子們為何如此的乖，肯乖乖地來做習題，其實是因為我偷偷地給他們糕餅和糖果吃的原因。他們的老師對我的賄賂行為，睜一隻眼，閉一隻眼，隨我怎麼辦。有一次，她告訴我糕餅內不可有花生，因為有一個小孩對花生過敏。

我當然對於我在南京的罪行感到無比的痛心。我買了一幢小的公寓，留了一筆錢，加上我當教授的退休金，我知道我可以活得安穩了。因此我將我的其餘財

---

assistant (n.) 助理   peanut (n.) 花生
lesson (n.) 課程   allergic (adj.) 對……過敏的
bribery (n.) 賄賂

neighborhood. I worked with a class of third graders on their mathematics homework at a study center. The children came up to me one by one, and I gave them exercises in mathematics to complete. In the beginning, a psychiatric assistant sat nearby. After a while, that stopped. I won't hide it from you that the reason the children were unusually well behaved for our lessons was that I secretly passed around cookies and candy. Their teacher noticed this bit of bribery I was up to. She turned a blind eye to it, and let me do what I pleased. What could be done about it? One time she told me to make sure there were no peanuts in the cookies. One of my little friends was allergic to peanuts.

Naturally I felt an incomparable sadness whenever I thought of my crimes at Nanjing. I bought a small apartment, deposited a bit of money in my academic retirement fund,

---

incomparable (adj.) 無可比擬的
apartment (n.) 公寓

deposit (v.) 存放、放置
fund (n.) 基金、資金

產，全部捐給了各種難民救援組織。我現在可以出去旅行了，可是我放棄了這個權利，我總要為我的罪行付出代價。

感謝上蒼我終於得到了心靈上的平安，四十多年來，我一直生活在恐懼之中。對絕大多數人而言，中日戰爭早就結束了。對我而言，這場戰爭，直到兩年前才結束。

看了木村教授的文章，又看到電視新聞中的各式各樣的衝突，我還是要問，為什麼人類永遠不會停止大屠殺呢？

——原載一九九九年六月十三日《聯合報》

---

the rest of 剩下的
property (n.) 財產
investment (n.) 投資

donate (v.) 捐獻
privilege (n.) 特權
means (n.) 方法、方式

enough, I knew, for a comfortable old age. I then took the
rest of my property and investments and donated the whole
of it to various disaster relief agencies. Now I am able to
travel, but I've given up the privilege. I have tried by every
means to pay for my crimes.

Thank the skies above that I have finally found peace
of mind. For over forty years, I lived in the grip of abject
terror. For the great majority of people, the Sino-Japanese
War ended long ago. As far as I am concerned, however,
that war raged on until just the last two years.

As I read Professor Kimura's words and thought of the
conflicts of every shape and sort that we see in daily
newscasts, a question comes to my mind. Why is it that
members of the human race seem so bent on butchering
one another?

---

abject (adj.) 悽慘的   conflict (n.) 衝突
majority (n.) 大多數   bent on 致力於
rage (v.) 肆虐、摧殘   butcher (v.) 屠戮

打不通的電話
The Telephone Call that Wouldn't Go through

鮑端磊　譯

　　我用刷卡進入了行政大樓，在辦公室裡辦了一些事。一小時以後，我發現大樓裡仍然安安靜靜的，怎麼會呢？通常到這個時候，行政大樓裡已經很多人了。我的祕書是從不遲到的，我的那位工讀生也從不遲到的。

I used my "swipe card" to let myself into the front door of the Administration Building. An hour passed and I realized the building was incredibly quiet. How could this be? Usually by this hour the building was full of people. My secretary had never been late before. My student assistant had never been late before.

前一陣子，因為處理震災的事情，我飽受攻擊，心裡當然很不舒服，非常希望別人來安慰我。夜深人靜，我更是常常打電話找人聊天，如果人家乘機安慰我幾句，我就感到非常舒服。

今天早上，我從暨南國際大學的校長宿舍開車去行政大樓。到達行政大樓的時候，發現大樓的門沒有打開。我看了一下錶，是早上七點半，也難怪那位每天來開門的工友還沒有來，可是我有一點訝異為什麼報紙也還沒有送來。

---

handle (v.) 處理
earthquake (n.) 地震
disaster (n.) 災難

pressure (n.) 壓力
relief (n.) 寬慰
residence (n.) 住所、住處

These past recent days, handling problems related to the earthquake disaster, I've really had my fill of troubles and pressure. It is only natural that I've been feeling uncomfortable and that I hoped so badly to receive comfort from others. Late into the night, I've made a number of telephone calls, just needing to talk. If anyone could offer a few words of comfort, I have felt great relief.

Early this morning, I drove from the residence of the president of Chinan International University to the Administration Building. When I arrived at the Administration Building, I found the front door had not been opened yet. I glanced at my wristwatch. It said it was 7:30 in the morning. It seemed odd that the worker who opened that door every day hadn't shown up yet. But I was also in for another surprise. Why hadn't the usual daily newspapers arrived?

---

president (n.) 校長
administration (n.) 行政

arrive (v.) 抵達
wristwatch (n.) 手錶

　　我用刷卡進入了行政大樓，在辦公室裡辦了一些事。一小時以後，我發現大樓裡仍然安安靜靜的，怎麼會呢？通常到這個時候，行政大樓裡已經很多人了。我的祕書是從不遲到的，我的那位工讀生也從不遲到的。

　　我等到了八點三刻，大樓裡仍然不見人影。我從窗子望出去，整個校園裡不見一個人影，也不見一輛車子。最奇怪的是：大門口的國旗也未見升起。我決定去看個究竟。我走出我的辦公室，到大樓的各處去張望一下，發現整個大樓裡沒有一個人。

　　我開車到了學生宿舍，宿舍的大門是關著的，可是也是虛掩而已。我進去了，發現整個學生宿舍人去樓

---

realize (v.) 了解、明白　　　　single (n.) 單一
incredibly (adv.) 難以相信地　　soul (n.) 靈魂；人
secretary (n.) 秘書　　　　　　the national flag 國旗
sign (n.) 跡象

I used my "swipe card" to let myself into the front door of the Administration Building. An hour passed and I realized the building was incredibly quiet. How could this be? Usually by this hour the building was full of people. My secretary had never been late before. My student assistant had never been late before.

I waited till 8:45 and still there was no sign of life in the building. I looked out my office window and I couldn't see a single soul or car anywhere on campus. The strangest thing of all was the national flag had not yet been hoisted on the flagpole. I decided to do a little investigating. I left my office. I looked all over that building. I found there wasn't a single person anywhere in sight.

I drove over to one of the student dormitories. The front entrance was closed, but it was not locked. I walked inside,

---

hoist (v.) 升起
flagpole (n.) 旗杆
investigate (v.) 調查

dormitory (n.) 宿舍
entrance (n.) 入口
lock (v.) 鎖住

空，每一張床上都沒有任何被褥；電腦、書籍、網球拍也都不見了，每一間寢室的櫃子裡都空空如也。走出宿舍，我發現停在宿舍門口的腳踏車、機車和汽車都不見了。

我到各個教學大樓去張望一下，每棟大樓前面都沒有一輛車子，我所能看到的只有一大群白鷺鷥。現在已是早上九點了，可是每間教室裡都是空的。

我去大門口的警衛室，發現那裡也是大門緊鎖。難怪國旗沒有升起來，可是我記得昨天我開車進校門的時候，還有一位警衛和我打招呼的。

---

empty (adj.) 空蕩蕩的
blanket (n.) 毯子
shelf (n.) 架子
closet (n.) 衣櫥

stroll (v.) 漫步、散步
vehicle (n.) 陸上交通工具、車輛
park (v.) 停放
flock (n.) 一群

and found the entire dormitory empty. There was no sign of blankets on the beds. There were no computers, book shelves or racks to be seen. The closet in every room was totally empty. As I strolled out of the dormitory, I saw no bicycles or motorcycles or cars near the entrance.

I went to the College of Education for a look around there, and couldn't find a single vehicle parked before any of the buildings. The only thing I could find was a flock of little egrets. It was nine o'clock in the morning at that point, and every classroom was empty.

At the guards' office in the front entrance of the university, the door was tightly locked. No wonder, I thought, that the national flag hadn't yet been raised. But I recalled how yesterday one of the guards waved a greeting my way as I passed through the entrance in my car.

---

egret (n.) 白鷺　　　　　　　　raise (v.) 升起
guard (n.) 守衛　　　　　　　　recall (v.) 回想
office (n.) 辦公室　　　　　　　wave (v.) 揮手致意
tightly (adv.) 很緊地　　　　　　greeting (n.) 問候

　　我忽然想起來，昨天晚上我回校園的時候，有一位老師的太太和我揮手致意，我趕緊開車到老師宿舍區去。令我感到好可怕的是：宿舍前一輛汽車也沒有。昨天晚上我還看到一大排車子停在那裡的，我還記得有很多小孩子在宿舍前面玩耍。現在，那些孩子也不見了，整個宿舍區看不到一個人影。

　　我只好回到我的辦公室去，在辦公室裡，我越來越難過。即使我處理震災處理得不太好，同學、老師和同仁們也不該這樣無情無義地對付我。現在已經是九點半，我決定打個電話給一位老朋友，希望他能安慰我幾句。我拿起電話聽筒，卻發現沒有表軌聲。我試了好幾

---

speed (v.) 疾駛　　　　　　district (n.) 區域、行政區
faculty (n.) 全體教員　　　weight (n.) 重量
throng (n.) 一大群　　　　respond (v.) 反應、回應

I suddenly thought of how when I returned to the campus the night before, the wife of a professor had waved at me. So, I sped to the faculty housing area. What really frightened me was that not even one car was parked there. The night before I had seen a bunch of cars parked in that spot. I remembered too the throng of children playing in front of the dormitory. Now those children were nowhere to be seen and there wasn't a sign of life in the entire housing district.

I headed back to my office and, once there, felt the weight of more and more sadness. If in handling the earthquake disaster, I had not responded so very well to the situation, still it was a fact the students and professors, my colleagues and so on should not have treated me so harshly, so unjustly. Now it was 9:30 a.m. I resolved to call an old friend. I hoped for a word of comfort from him.

---

treat (v.) 對待
harshly (adv) 嚴厲地
unjustly (adv) 不公平地

resolve (v.) 決定
comfort (n.) 慰藉

次，都是如此。

打開收音機，沒有任何電台可以聽。

打開電視機，沒有任何電視台可看。

我當時願意以我的一切來換取別人給我的一點安
慰，可是顯然不可能了。

我忽然想起了一件事。我想起我們學務處裡的一位
職員，他的房子全垮了，八百萬的家產一夜之間泡了
湯，他自己也是從瓦礫堆中爬出來的。我想他一定也渴
望有人安慰他，可是我一直因為事情太忙而沒有親自去

---

receiver (n.) 電話聽筒 　　　　　moment (n.) 時刻

I picked up the receiver and found there was no dial tone. I tried several times, but that was the way it was.

I turned on the radio. There was no radio station to listen to.

I turned on the television. There was no TV station to watch.

In those moments I'd have given all I had for someone to give me a little comfort, but clearly that was simply impossible.

Then all of a sudden something came to my mind. I thought of a clerk in the academic affairs office. His house had collapsed, a residence worth eight million Taiwan dollars had gone down the tube like dishwater, and he himself had pawed his way out from beneath the

---

collapse (v.) 倒塌

安慰他。經過今天早上的經驗，我更瞭解他的心情。我
決定打個電話給他。

　　我伸手去拿電話筒，猶豫了一下，電話是不是會依
然不通？可是，我仍然要試試看。令我驚異的是：電話
通了。我的同事正準備開車來上班，他對我的關心，感
到十分的快樂。

　　我又想起一位學生，他的媽媽病重，我決定打個電
話去問他情形如何。這一次，電話又通了。就在我結束

---

ruin (n.) 廢墟　　　　　　　tile (n.) 瓦
bury (v.) 掩埋　　　　　　　assorted (adj.) 各式各樣
brick (n.) 磚　　　　　　　rubble (n.) 瓦礫

ruins, nearly buried in bricks, tiles and assorted rubble. It occurred to me that he surely longed for people to comfort him. But because I had been too busy with all I had to do, I hadn't personally extended a shred of comfort to him. Having been through this experience that morning, I had a clearer understanding of his suffering. I decided to call him.

I reached for the telephone receiver, and then put it back down. The call wouldn't be able to go through, would it? But I wanted to try anyway. The telephone rang. That really caught me off guard. My colleague was just getting ready to climb into his car to come to work. He was so happy to see that I was concerned about him.

I also thought of a student whose mother had been seriously ill. I decided to give him a call to check on his situation. This time again, the call went through. Just as I

---

extend (v.) 給予
shred (n.) 少量
suffering (n.) 痛苦

off guard 沒提防
concerned (adj.) 擔憂、關心
seriously (adv.) 嚴重地

通話的時候，一位工讀生走了進來。我對他說：「小
子，你難道不知道現在已經十點了嗎？」我的工讀生一
臉困惑的表情。他指著牆上的鐘，對我說：「李校長，
您說什麼？」我回過頭去，發現只有七點半。

　　我站了起來，從窗子看出去，發現國旗已升了起
來。校園裡有一些汽車和機車開來開去，也有一位身體
強壯的男生在慢跑。

　　我抓了那位工讀生，叫他陪我去學生宿舍區，發現
宿舍裡大多數學生在呼呼大睡。已經起來的同學紛紛和
我打招呼。我又跑去找警衛，他們歡迎我進去喝茶。我

---

conversation (n.) 對話　　　　　sweep (v.) 掠過
confusion (n.) 困惑　　　　　　spot (v.) 發現

was ending that conversation, a student assistant strolled in. I said to him, "Young man, don't you know it's already 10 o'clock?" A look of confusion swept over the student's face. He pointed to the clock on the wall and said to me, "President Lee? What did you just say?" I turned around and looked, and saw it was only 7:30.

I stood up and looked out the window. I discovered the flag had been raised. Cars and motorcycles were buzzing around campus. I spotted a strong, burly young fellow out for a jog.

I grabbed the student assistant and told him to go with me to the student dormitory district. I found most of the students fast asleep. A smattering of students already up and about waved and greeted me. I dashed over to the guards' gate. They invited me to drink morning tea with

---

burly (adj.) 結實、魁梧　　　grab (v.) 抓住
jog (n.) 慢跑　　　smattering (n.) 少數

去老師宿舍區，看到好多老師們正在送孩子上學，有一位老師太太還請我進他們家去吃早餐。

我的工讀生完全不懂這是怎麼一個事。我無法告訴他我的經驗。他太年輕，不會懂的。我決定將我這個神奇的經驗寫下來，將來他如果有一天渴望別人安慰他的時候，很可能發現電話不通，好友盡去，他不妨想想別人的不幸遭遇，而且設法去安慰別人。到那個時候，他會發現電話通了，好友也都回來了。

——原載二〇〇〇年二月十七日《聯合報》

---

dispatch (v.) 派遣、發送　　　　in the dark 不知道

them. I went to the faculty housing area and saw that many colleagues were busy dispatching their children to schools. The wife of a professor invited me to sit down at their family table for breakfast.

My student assistant was completely in the dark about all this business. He was too young, and had no way to understand it. I resolved to put this amazing experience into writing. In the future, if he would ever have a day when he hoped other folks would offer a little comfort to him, he'd be sure to find the dial tone on his telephone receiver silent and his friends nowhere to be seen. He would be wise to find a way to give comfort to someone else. All he need do was find a way to show some comfort to someone else. That would be the moment of the great discovery. His telephone would ring and his true friends would all come back to him.

---

wise (adj.) 明智

窮人的遺囑
A Poor Man's Will

康士林　譯

　　老神父當年叮囑他愛人，然後說將財產遺給他，老神父的財產就是心靈上的平安，心靈上的平安不是白白地能得到的，只有真心愛人的人，才能擁有它，老神父的意思是：「年輕神父，你如能真正的愛人，就能得到心靈上的平安。」

　　At that time, the old priest had ordered him to love others so that he could get his inheritance, which was nothing but peace in the heart. It was not something that could be gotten for free. One had to have the heart to love others before this peace could be had. The intention of the old priest was: Young priest, if you could really love people, you could get peace of mind.

我做律師已經快三十年了，當然常要處理遺產的事，通常需要律師處理遺產的人，多半是有錢的人，可是我曾經處理一個案件，寫遺囑的人卻是一個沒有多少遺產的神父。

這是二十年前的事，一位在南投縣鄉下的年輕神父寫信給我，他說，他們那裡的老神父病重，需要一位律師去見證他的遺囑，我信天主教，他們請我去，當然希望我能免費服務。

身為天主教徒，我覺得這件事義不容辭，立刻就去了。老神父雖然病重，卻不願住院，住在教堂裡。我去的時候，他很清醒，但非常虛弱，已經不能說話，遺囑

---

lawyer (n.) 律師　　　　　　possession (n.) 財產
will (n.) 遺囑　　　　　　　witness (v.) 簽名作證

I've been a lawyer for about thirty years and have of course handled many wills. Ordinarily the majority of those wanting a lawyer to make a will are wealthy. But once I handled the case of a priest who wanted to write a will but didn't have many possessions.

This was something from twenty years ago. A young priest from the countryside in Nantou County had written me saying that they had an old priest who was seriously ill and who wanted a lawyer to witness his will. I'm a Catholic so they probably invited me to go naturally hoping I would work for free.

As a Catholic, I felt that this was something I could not refuse and immediately went there. Although the old priest was quite sick, he was not willing to go to the hospital and was living at the church. He was wide awake when I went

---

for free 免費
refuse (v.) 拒絕

willing (adj.) 有意願的
awake (adj.) 醒著的

大概是他口述以後，別人寫的。

　　這一份遺囑的主要內容都是對那位新的年輕神父寫
的，老神父在遺囑中叮囑新神父好多事情，比方說，有
一位教友最近失業了，情緒很不穩定，老神父請新神父
一定要去幫助他找一份工作；某某人酗酒，老神父叮囑
新神父幫助他戒酒；某某國中學生不想念書，成天混，
老神父希望新神父好好地管教這個小孩子；某某年輕人
在台中打工，有參加幫派的可能，老神父請新神父務必

---

weak (adj.) 虛弱的　　　　　　　a great many 很多
urge (v.) 勸、催促　　　　　　　unemployed (adj.) 失業的

there but very weak, not even able to talk. The will was probably written down by some one else after the priest had told him what to say.

The content of the will was written for that new, young priest. In the will, the old priest urged the new priest to do a great many things. For example, there was a Catholic who was recently unemployed and emotionally unstable. The old priest urged the new priest definitely to help this Catholic find work. So and so was drinking too much; the old priest urged the new one to help this person give up drinking. A certain junior high school student who didn't want to study was fooling around all day long. The old priest hoped that new one would take this child under his wing. Then there was the young man working in Taichung who was probably involved with a gang. The old priest asked the new priest to make sure that this young man

---

emotionally (adv.) 情緒上
unstable (adj.) 不穩定的

fool around 閒混
involved (adj.) 牽扯其中的

要使這位年輕人不致誤入歧途。我記得大概有七個案例，老神父一再叮囑新神父一定要認真照顧他們。

遺囑的最後一句話是「我的財產全部遺給張神父」，張神父就是那位新來的年輕神父。

我將遺囑念了一遍，問老神父是不是的確寫了這份遺囑，老神父點了點頭，他已經無法簽字了，我們拉著他的手指畫了押，如此就完成了手續。

幾天以後，張神父告訴我，老神父過世了，我告訴他遺囑已經開始生效。我當時好奇，問他究竟老神父有

---

astray (adv.) 迷路；偏離正軌　　　emphatically (adv.) 強調地

would not go astray. I remember that there were probably seven cases that the old priest emphatically urged the new priest to take care of for sure and with much seriousness.

The last sentence in the will was "I leave all of my possessions to Fr. Chang." Fr. Chang is the name of the newly-arrived young priest.

I read over the will and asked the old priest if he had really written this. He could only nod his head since he was already not able to write. We held his hand as he made a fingerprint, and, in this way, brought the process to an end.

A few days afterwards, Fr. Chang informed me that the old priest had passed away. I told him that the will had

---

fingerprint (n.) 指印、指紋　　　pass away 過世

多少財產。新神父告訴我說，他們發現他遺有現款二百元新台幣，還有一些舊衣物和書，即使在二十年前，二百元實在不算什麼，老神父顯然是個不折不扣的窮人，新神父從老神父那裡好像沒有得到任何遺產。

　　我每年都會收到張神父的一份報告書，說明他如何處理那七個案子，看來他處理得不錯，也都有好結果。四年以後，我告訴他，他已經照神父的遺囑做了，以後不需要再送報告過來了，這個案子就此結束。

---

in effect 生效　　　　　　　amount (v.) 合計達
curiosity (n.) 好奇心　　　　genuine (adj.) 真的、真誠的
reply (v.) 回答

already started to be in effect. Out of curiosity, I asked him exactly how many possessions the old priest had. The new priest replied that they discovered that he had 200 NT in cash and some old clothes and books. Even though this was twenty years ago, the 200 NT didn't amount to much money. The old priest obviously was a genuine poor person. The new priest, it seems, didn't get any inheritance from the old one.

Each year I would receive a report from Fr. Chang explaining how he had handled those seven cases. It seemed that he handled them very well and that each one had a good end. After four years, I told him that he had already accomplished the provisions of the old priest's will and that he did not need to send me any further reports. And so my work regarding this will came to an end.

---

inheritance (n.) 遺產
accomplish (v.) 達成

provision (n.) 條款
regarding (prep.) 關於

　　二十年過去了，我的祕書在整理檔案時發現了這個案件，也勾起了我再度去南投鄉下的想法，我設法聯絡上那位當時年輕的張神父，他仍在那裡，我說我想去看他，他十分地表示歡迎。

　　二十年前，我就覺得鄉下這裡好舒服，空氣新鮮，風景好，又沒有交通擁擠，現在這種好感更加強烈了，當時的年輕神父現在已經步入中年，他一方面招呼我坐下，一方面仍在應付許多事情，我感覺到這個小村落的每個人都是他要照顧的，他和我談話不到幾分鐘，就會有人來找他。

　　我們談了一陣子，我決定問張神父一個問題，以解

---

tempt (v.) 誘使　　　　　　　　comfortable (adj.) 舒適的
figure out 想出

With the passing of twenty years, my secretary, in going through my files, discovered this case, which tempted me to think about going down to the Nantou countryside again. I figured out a way to contact Fr. Chang, who had been young then. He was still there and I said that I wanted to see him. He expressed a very warm welcome.

Twenty years ago, I had felt how comfortable the countryside was: fresh air, beautiful scenery, no traffic congestion. Now the same good feeling was even stronger. The previously young priest was now in his middle age. The same time he was telling me to take a seat, he was also taking care of many other things. I had the feeling that he took care of every person in this little village. Whenever we had talked for a few minutes, someone came to see him.

We talked for a while and then I decided to ask Fr. Chang

---

congestion (n.) 擁塞   previously (adv.) 先前

我的心頭疑問。我問他那位老神父明明知道他只有二百元新台幣，為什麼要在遺囑中說他要將財產遺給他？張神父說他當時也不懂，他以為老神父老來糊塗了。可是幾年以後，他終於懂了。他說他當時才從美國念完碩士回國，他畢業於美國的明星大學，碩士學位是生物化學，總以為自己會被派到大學去輔導大學生，沒有想到被派到山間的鄉下，他說這裡的教友根本對他的學問毫無興趣，他因此有些不安，也有點失望。

---

clarify (v.) 釐清
return (v.) 返回

famous (adj.) 有名的
biochemisity (n.) 生物化學

a question so as to clarify something on my mind. I asked him why that respected old priest, who clearly knew he had only had 200 NT, would have said in his will that he wanted to give his possessions to him. Fr. Chang said that at the time he too did not understand. He thought the old priest might have just been confused. But after a few years, he at last understood. He said that at that time he had just returned from the United States with an M.A. degree. He had graduated from a famous American university and his degree was in biochemistry. Originally, he had thought that he would be assigned to work at a university as a student counselor. He had not thought that he would be sent to the country-side up in the mountains. He said that the parishioners here had not the least interest in his learning. Because of this he was not at peace and was a bit disappointed.

---

assign (v.) 分配、指派　　　　　disappointed (adj.) 失望的
parishioner (n.) 教區住民

　　可是他規規矩矩地照老神父的遺囑做了，一旦開始，他就全心投入了關懷村民的工作，他發現有好多人需要他的幫助，他也就成天幫助他們。有一天，他忽然發現，他擁有一個特別的東西，就是心靈上的平安，而他知道，如果他沒有愛人，他是不會有這種平安的。

　　老神父當年叮囑他愛人，然後說將財產遺給他，老神父的財產就是心靈上的平安，心靈上的平安不是白白地能得到的，只有真心愛人的人，才能擁有它，老神父的意思是：「年輕神父，你如能真正的愛人，就能得到心靈上的平安。」

　　神父告訴我，他仍和他的老同學、老朋友有聯絡。

---

obediently (adv.) 服從地　　　　　look after 照看、照料

Nonetheless, he obediently carried out the will of the old priest. Once he started, he threw himself heart and soul into the work of looking after the villagers. He soon realized that a great many people needed his help. All day long he was helping them. Then, one day, he suddenly discovered that he had something that was very special: peace in his heart. He further understood that if he had not loved others, he would not have been able to have this peace.

At that time, the old priest had ordered him to love others so that he could get his inheritance, which was nothing but peace in the heart. It was not something that could be gotten for free. One had to have the heart to love others before this peace could be had. The intention of the old priest was: Young priest, if you could really love people, you could get peace of mind.

Fr. Chang told me that he was still in contact with his

---

in contact with 有連絡

他們也都常常來看他，和他們比起來，他的確看上去一無所有，但是他所感到的平安，卻不是他那些同學所能享受的。

我們天主教徒，個個想得平安，但真正心中有平安的人是很少的，為什麼？無非是因為我們沒有抓到祕訣，我們應該知道，平安絕非白白地能夠得到的，沒有愛人是不能享受這份珍貴寶物的。

我開車回台北的時候，決定要將那份遺囑好好地保存起來，因為它所牽涉到的是一份無比巨大的財產，最重要的是：寫遺囑的人過世的時候，一無所有，是個道道地地的窮人。

——原載二〇〇三年一月十八日《聯合報》

old classmates and friends. They all often came to see him. When he compared himself with them, indeed looked as if he had nothing. But the peace he experienced was something that they did not enjoy.

We Catholics all think of getting peace, but those who really have peace are very few. Why? It must be because we have not grasped the secret: we need to know that peace is not something gotten for free. If we don't love others, we cannot enjoy this precious gift.

When I was driving back to Taipei, I decided to preserve very carefully that will, because it was about an incomparably immense possession. Most importantly, the one who had written the will had nothing when he died: he was truly a poor person.

---

preserve (v.) 保存　　　　　immense (adj.) 龐大的

大庇天下阿強俱歡顏
May every "A-Chiang" in the World be Blessed with a Smiling Face

康士林　譯

　　有一天，有人敲我研究室的門，開了門，門口站著的是阿強，這次他穿得整整齊齊的，除了牛仔褲和白色球鞋以外，他出我意料之外地穿了一件白色的長袖襯衫，一望而知，這件襯衫是全新的。

One day, there was a knock on the door of my study. Opening the door, I saw A-Chiang standing there. This time he was very neatly dressed. Besides wearing jeans and white tennis shoes, much to my surprise, he was wearing a white, long-sleeved shirt. At a glance, I knew it was brand new.

學校裡常有些工程在進行，工人多半年輕，但工頭卻常常是年紀大的人，物以類聚，年紀大的工頭當然會喜歡找我這種老頭子聊天。

大概四年前吧！有一位叫趙老闆的工頭到我的研究室來閒話家常，他告訴我他沒有受過什麼教育，只有小學畢業，但是他們夫婦倆省吃儉用，將兩個兒子都送進了大學。所以他現在可以無憂無慮了，因為兩個兒子都有了好的工作。

談到念書，他忽然問我，什麼叫做「浪淘盡千古風流人物」，這下我可慘了，因為我發現，他根本不知道

---

under construction 工事中　　　shoot the breeze 閒聊
foreman (n.) 工頭　　　　　　gab (v.) 瞎聊

Our school often has places under construction. Most of the workers are young and the foreman often is an older man. Since "birds of a feather flock together," the old foreman naturally likes to look for me and shoot the breeze with me, another old guy.

It must have been about four years ago. One of the foremen called Boss Chao came to my study and we gabbed about family things. He told me that he had not received much education, only graduating from elementary school. But both he and his wife were thrifty regarding living expenses, and they were able to send their two sons to college. Now they had no worries at all because the two sons had good work.

In talking about studying, he suddenly asked me, "What is the meaning of 'The waves carrieth away thousands

thrifty (adj.) 節儉的
living expenses生活費

suddenly (adv.) 突然

這句話裡面的字是怎麼寫的，只是知道這句話的音而已，我用盡了方法，將前後文結結巴巴地解釋了好一陣子，趙老闆似懂非懂地點了點頭，其實我想他大概是一知半解的。

我問趙老闆從哪裡聽來這句話的，他說他是從阿強那裡聽來的。他說阿強是他手下的工人，也是個怪人，常常在休息的時候喃喃自語，而且聲音很大。起先大家都以為他精神有問題，後來才知道阿強喜歡古詩古詞，他會背一大堆的古詩古詞，休息的時候，他就大聲地背那些古詩古詞，「浪淘盡千古風流人物」，是阿強常常

haltingly (adv.) 吞吞吐吐地　　classical (adj.) 古典的
mumble (v.) 含糊地說

of gallants'"? For a moment I was struck dumb, for I discovered that he didn't know at all how to write the Chinese characters for this line of verse. He only knew how to say it. For some time, I used as many ways as possible to explain haltingly this line to him. Boss Chao kept nodding his head as if he understood; actually I thought he probably understood little of it.

I asked Boss Chao where he had heard this expression. He said he had heard it from A-Chiang, who was a worker under him and was somewhat strange. When A-Chiang would take a rest, he would often be mumbling to himself, and the sound was very loud. At first everyone thought that he had some mental problem. Afterwards everyone knew that A-Chiang liked classical Chinese poetry, of which he had memorized a great deal. During a break he would loudly recite poetry. "The waves carrieth away

---

memorize (v.) 背熟　　　　　　recite (v.) 朗誦

口中念念有詞的句子，趙老闆最後也記得了這個句子了。趙老闆還記得一句阿強常常念的句子，「小樓昨夜又東風」，他說他比較能體會這個句子的意義。

我對阿強大為有興趣，很想看看這位工人是何模樣，趙老闆答應替我去請他來找我，不過他說沒有把握阿強肯來。

過了一陣子，我聽到了敲門聲，開了門，我看到了這位喜歡古詩古詞的阿強。

我心目中的阿強大概是工人中比較文雅的一類，可是我現在看到的阿強又黑又壯，因為是夏天，他光了上

---

original (adj.) 起初的　　　　　comparatively (adv.) 比較地

thousands of gallants" was a line of poetry that was often on his lips, which in turn made Boss Chao memorize this line. He had also memorized another line which A-Chiang also often recited: "Last night the little room again felt the east wind." He said that for this line he somewhat understood the meaning.

I became very interested in A-Chiang and wanted to see what he was like. Boss Chao agreed to arrange for him to come and see me, but he was not sure if A-Chiang would be willing.

After a while, I heard a knock on my door, and saw this A-Chiang who liked to recite classical poetry.

My original thought was that A-Chiang was probably a comparatively refined worker. But the A-Chiang I saw was dark and muscular. Because it was summer he was bare-

---

refined (adj.) 文雅   muscular (adj.) 健壯

身，不僅渾身是汗，而且整個身體都是泥土和水泥之類
的東西。至於他的表情呢？這倒是很容易形容，他的表
情就是「不情不願」。還沒有開口說話，我已經知道他
想說「你這個糟老頭找我來幹嘛 ？」

　　我沒有等他開口說話，就問他是不是阿強呢？他嗯
了一聲，我請他進來坐下，他自己感到很不自在，一來
我的冷氣好像對他是太冷了一點，還有一點，他有點怕
將我的研究室的椅子坐髒了。

　　一開始阿強和我聊天，全部都是「長問短答」。儘
管我使出渾身解數來使他感到我有迷人之處，他就是懶

---

sweaty (adj.) 全身是汗　　　　describe (v.) 描述
cover (v.) 覆蓋　　　　　　　　nasty (adj.) 討厭的
cement (n.) 水泥

chested. Not only was he all sweaty but his entire body was covered with dirt and cement. As for his expression? This is easy to describe. He had come "most unwillingly." Even before he spoke, I knew that he wanted to say "What the hell did you call me here for you nasty old man?"

I didn't wait for him to open his mouth and just asked him if he were A-Chiang. He mumbled he was and I asked him to come in and sit down. He himself felt very uncomfortable. On the one hand it seemed that the air conditioning was a little too cold for him, and on the other, he was a bit afraid that he would dirty the chair in my study.

At the beginning of our talk, it was all short answers to long questions. Even though I tried to do everything to get him to feel my engaging personality, he still appeared

---

air conditioning 空調
afraid (adj.) 害怕的

dirty (v.) 弄髒
engaging (adj.) 迷人的

得和我聊天。可是他忽然看到我桌上的《讓高牆倒下吧！》那本書，問我是不是李家同，我說我就是，這一下他忽然變了一個人。

他說他在小學六年級的時候，曾經得過一次獎，獎品就是《讓高牆倒下吧！》，他也從此知道在新竹縣寶山鄉的德蘭中心，他知道我在那裡做家教，他鄰居有一家的小孩子全部都在德蘭中心，其中一位是我學生，這個小鬼每次回去都會吹噓他功課多好，雖然他是小學生，英文卻已經很好了。

阿強請我將冷氣關小一點，因為他渾身是汗，冷氣吹在汗上，非常不舒服，而且他說他習慣了在烈日之下

---

reluctant (adj.) 不情願的　　　　brat (n.) 小傢伙

reluctant to talk. Then suddenly he saw the book *Let the High Wall Fall* on my desk and asked me if I were Li Chia-tung. I said I was, and all of a sudden he became totally different.

He said that in the sixth grade he had once won an award, and the prize was the book *Let the High Wall Fall*. From this book he had learned about the Theresian Center in the town of Baoshan in Hsinchu County. He knew that I was a tutor there. One of the families in his neighborhood had all of their children at the Theresian Center, one of whom was my student. This little brat would brag about how good his grades were each time he returned home. Even though he was an elementary school student, his English was already very good.

A-Chiang asked me to turn down the air-conditioning because he was all sweaty. It was very uncomfortable to

---

brag (v.) 吹噓

揮汗如雨地工作，幾乎很少有吹冷氣的機會。我唯命是從地照做了。以後，阿強的話匣子就打開了。

　　阿強小學在尖石鄉念的，他有一位非常好的老師，一直強迫他們大量閱讀，現在他回想起來，班上的圖書大概都是由這位老師自己掏腰包買的，這位老師還強迫學生背古詩古詞，因為他從小就體格高大，因此老師就指定他為小老師，所有的同學都要背給他聽，當然他一定要先會背才行，班上雖然不到十位同學，但是他每次都要聽很多次背誦，日久天長就會背很多古詩詞了。

---

rare (adj.) 罕見　　　　　　　　continually (adv.) 持續地

have the cold air blowing on his sweat. He also said that he was already accustomed to working with the sweat pouring out of him like rain. It was most rare for him to have the chance for air-conditioning. I did what I was told to do. Afterwards, he became a talking machine.

The elementary school that A-Chiang had gone to was in the town of Chianshih. He had an exceptionally good teacher who continually forced them to read much. As he thought of it, most likely all of the books for the class came out of the pocket of that teacher. This teacher also forced the students to memorize classical poetry. Because A-Chiang was big for his age, the teacher made him the "little teacher." All of the students had to recite poetry for A-Chiang, so of course he had first to memorize the poem. Although there were not even ten students in the class, he still had each time to listen to the recitation a number of times. As the time passed, he was able to memorize many

---

force (v.) 強迫

　　這位老師使阿強從小就喜歡文學，他一直在班上功課很好。不幸的是，小學六年級的時候，他父親因為工地發生意外而喪生了，他的媽媽帶了他和他的弟弟搬到了城裡來。這一個變故，他忽然感受到了貧困是怎麼一回事。有好幾次，他幾乎晚上只有白飯，而沒有什麼菜吃。他的家斷水斷電，更是經常發生的事。

　　尤其令他傷心的是他的功課完全跟不上，英文情形最嚴重。他小時在鄉下，小學裡英文根本沒有學，開始

---

perform (v.) 表現　　　　　　accident (n.) 意外事故
due to 由於　　　　　　　　　site (n.) 地點

poems.

This teacher was responsible for A-Chiang, who always performed very well in class, to love literature since his childhood. Unfortunately, when he was in the sixth grade, his father lost his life due to an accident at a construction site, and his mother took him and his little brother to the city to live. With this change, he suddenly realized the real meaning of poverty. On many occasions, for supper, they only had rice and no vegetables to eat. The water and electricity at his home were often cut off, which then became a common occurrence.

What hurt him the most was that he couldn't keep up with his classmates in studies, the most serious problem being English. As a child in the country-side, he simply didn't study any English in elementary school. When he

poverty (n.) 貧困   common (adj.) 常見的

上城裡國中的時候，連ABC都不認識，但是他的同班同學卻已經認識了好多英文字，他怎麼樣也跟不上，老師每週小考一次，他永遠是班上最後一名，也永遠被老師罵，每次都被罰站一小時。

　　他發現他的同班同學之所以英文好，絕非聰明，而是家境比他好的緣故，有些同學的父母英文非常好，另外一批同學不是家裡有家教，就是上補習班，他媽媽英文一個字也不會，他的長輩也都不會英文，當然也無法進補習班和請家教。他在國中一年級上學期還念了一下英文，下學期就放棄了。

catch up 跟上、趕上　　　　criticize (v.) 批評
quiz (n.) 小考　　　　　　　punish (v.) 處罰

started junior high school in the city, he didn't even know his ABCs. His classmates, however, already knew many English words. No matter what he did, he couldn't catch up and he was always the last in the class for the weekly English quiz. The teacher always criticized him, and he was punished by having to stand in the corner for an hour.

He discovered that his classmates' English was good not because they were especially intelligent, but because their families were better off than his. Some classmates' parents knew English very well. Other classmates, if they didn't have an English tutor, went to a remedial school for English. His mother, however, didn't know a word of English, nor did any of his older generation. He didn't have any chance to go to a remedial school or get a tutor. For his first semester in junior high school, he still studied some English, but in the next semester he gave up.

---

better off 處境更好
remedial (adj.) 改善的、矯正的

generation (n.) 世代
semester (n.) 學期

數學也是如此，他只是會做教科書裡的習題，可是
考試題目就不會了。後來他發現那些考試的題目其實可
以在一些參考書裡看到的，但他沒有錢買參考書，所以
數學成績也相當不好。

在一年級下學期的時候，阿強完全放棄了升高中的
希望，他知道他絕對考不上公立學校，至於私立學校，
他一定付不起學費，所以他就決心找工作來做。

當時他只有國中一年級，但是他體格高大，這給他

---

exercise (n.) 練習題　　　　　supplementary (adj.) 補充的
examination (n.) 考試　　　　　reference book 參考書

Mathematics was also like this. He could only do the exercises in the textbook, but he couldn't do the questions on the examinations. Later he discovered that the questions on the exams were actually in some supplementary reference books but he didn't have any money to buy them. As a result, his math grades were not very good either.

During the second semester of his first year, A-Chiang gave up any hope of going on to high school. He knew that he had absolutely no hope of passing the exam for a public high school. As for a private high school, he wouldn't be able to pay the tuition. He therefore determined to find a job.

At that time, even though he was a first-year junior high school student, he was tall and strong, which allowed him

---

as a result 結果是
private (adj.) 私人的、私立的

tuition (n.) 學費
determine (v.) 決定

找到了一個在建築工地暑假打工的機會，工頭就是趙老闆，趙老闆發現他沒有父親，幾乎將他看成自己的兒子，除了給他打工的機會以外，還對他管教甚嚴。

當時有人給他機會去販賣盜版光碟，他也真的做了，被趙老闆知道，將他臭罵了一頓，他想如果他不是大個子，早就挨打了。也虧得如此，他才沒有被警察抓去。他有一個朋友，現在就在一所感化院裡服刑，罪名是「違反著作權法」。說到這裡，阿強難掩不滿之情，因為他不懂警察為什麼不去抓那些製造盜版光碟的人，而要拿這些窮小孩子來開刀。

---

pirated (adj.) 盜版的
scold (v.) 責罵

forcefully (adv.) 強而有力地
beat (v.) 打

to find work on a construction site during the summer vacation. The foreman was Boss Chao, who, when he learned that A-Chiang had no father, treated him like his own son. Besides giving him a chance to work, he also carefully disciplined him.

At that time he was given a chance to sell pirated CD's on the street, which he did. When Boss Chao found out, he scolded him forcefully. If he hadn't been so large, A-Chiang probably would have been beaten. Fortunately in this way he wasn't caught by the police. He had a friend who's now serving in a reform school; his crime was "Breaking the Copyright Law." When he got this far, A-Chiang couldn't cover up his anger, because he didn't understand why the police didn't go after the ones who made the pirated copies but instead took it out on poor kids like them.

---

reform school 少年感化院   cover up 掩飾

　　從此以後，趙老伯就一直設法給阿強臨時工做，薪水不錯，唯一的條件是他不能學壞，不能喝酒，不能抽菸，不能嚼檳榔，不能打架，當然不能和任何黑道人士接觸，阿強發現他不再有挨餓的日子，水電也沒有斷過。

　　阿強知道自己升學已經無望，但他的弟弟當時還在小學，所以就設法湊了一些錢，將他的弟弟送進了補習班，他和趙老伯商量，由趙老伯設立了一個帳戶，裡面的錢全部都是替他弟弟準備的補習費用。

　　在阿強和我聊天的那一年，他的弟弟讀國中二年

---

part-time (adj.) 兼職的　　　　　chew (v.) 咀嚼
salary (n.) 薪水　　　　　　　　gang (n.) 幫派

Afterwards, Uncle Chao always came up with a way to give him part-time work with a good salary. The only conditions were: he was not to learn anything bad; he was not to drink, smoke or chew beetle-nut; he was not to fight; and he was especially not to have anything to do with gangs. A-Chiang no longer had to go hungry, and the water and electricity were no longer cut off.

A-Chiang knew there was no chance of his going to senior high school, but his younger brother was still in elementary school, so he came up with a way to gather a little money to send his brother to remedial school. He discussed the matter with Uncle Chao, who opened a bank account in which all the money he put there would be used for his brother's education.

As A-Chiang and I were talking, he said that his brother

---

come up with 想出   account (n.) 帳戶

級，他說他的弟弟念書毫無問題，永遠是班上的前三名，考上明星高中也絕不是問題，而他呢？他十七歲已是有相當技術水準的水泥工人，趙老闆一直教他一些絕活，使他的薪水越來越高。他當然羨慕那些升上了高中的同學們，有一次，他在工地做工，同學們騎腳踏車經過，親熱地和他打招呼，也停下來和他聊天，他們都穿了高中制服，他只穿了一件汗衫，而且上面全是灰，他感到很不好意思。他們同學聚會，他去過一次，後來就不去了。雖然同學們對他很好，他卻很不自在。

雖然阿強的數學和英文等等都不好，他對國文卻一

---

skilled (adj.)有技巧、熟練的　　　　envy (v.) 羨慕

was now in the second year of junior high school and had no trouble whatsoever with his school work. He was always among the top three of the class and would have no trouble getting into a famous senior high school. As for A-Chiang? At seventeen, he was already a skilled cement worker. Boss Chao taught him some special skills, and made his pay more and more. A-Chiang of course envied those of his classmates who had passed the exam for senior high school. One day, when he was working at a construction site, his classmates passed on bicycles and warmly called out to him. They stopped and talked with him. They were wearing their school uniforms, and he was in a T-shirt covered with dust, which was most embarrassing. He went once to a class gathering, but never went again. Even though his classmates were all nice to him, he was not all that comfortable.

Even though A-Chiang's English, math, and so on were

---

uniform (n.) 制服   embarrassing (adj.) 感到尷尬的

直都有興趣，他也常常去學校圖書館借書看，我寫的書他都看過了，令我「龍心大悅」，趕快拿了很多糕點和冷飲請他享用。

我送阿強回工地去，他沒有用電梯，而是走樓梯下去，我發現他是赤腳的。在走樓梯下去的時候，阿強希望我成立一個機構，專門替窮小孩子找家教。他說窮小孩子的功課不好，大多是因為回了家沒有人問。

我雖然答應阿強會注意他的建議，但是當時我心想我哪有能力成立這個機構，除非我碰到了一個善心的富

---

maintain (v.) 保持
library (n.) 圖書館

pleased (adj.) 滿意的、開心的
emperor (n.) 皇帝

not good, he still maintained interest in Chinese literature, often going to the school's library to read. He had read all of my books, which made myself very pleased "with the pride of an emperor." I immediately gave him some cakes and a cold drink to enjoy.

I saw A-Chiang off to his construction site. He didn't take the elevator but the steps. I saw that he was bare-footed. As we were walking down the steps, A-Chiang said he hoped that I could establish an agency whose job would be to find tutors for poor kids. Poor kids, he said, are not good in their studies mainly because when they go home there is no one to ask questions to.

Even though I agreed to take care of A-Chiang's suggestion, at that time I thought to myself how could I ever be able to set up such an agency, unless I ran into a

---

bare-footed (adj.) 赤腳的　　　　suggestion (n.) 建議
take care of 關注、注意

翁。

　　就這麼巧，有一位心腸很好的有錢人來找我。他有錢，也很想回饋社會，但不知如何去做？我逮到了這個機會，勸他成立一個專門替弱勢孩子補習的基金會，他立刻答應了。這就是博幼基金會，已經成立了一年多了。好多弱勢孩子受了惠，只是這位善心人士始終不肯露面。

　　我寫信告訴阿強這個消息，他回信來了。短短的幾句話，除了表示高興以外，也告訴我一個好消息，他的弟弟進入了一所相當著名的高中。

---

philanthropic (adj.) 慈善的　　　　on the spot 當場
disadvantaged (adj.) 弱勢的　　　　in operation 運作中

philanthropic wealthy person.

Quite incidentally, a weathly man with a good heart came to see me. He had money and wanted to give some back to society, but didn't know what to do. I seized this opportunity to urge him to set up a foundation that would help disadvantaged children to get remedial education. He agreed on the spot. This is now the Boyo Social Welfare Foundation, which has been in operation for already over a year. Many disadvantaged children have already benefited from this foundation, but this good-hearted founder has never been willing to have his identity revealed.

I wrote a letter to A-Chiang about this news, and he replied with a few words expressing not only his happincss for this but also telling me some good news: his brother had entered a very good senior high school.

---

benefit (v.) 受惠於
founder (n.) 創始人

reveal (v.) 洩漏

　　有一天，有人敲我研究室的門，開了門，門口站著
的是阿強，這次他穿得整整齊齊的，除了牛仔褲和白色
球鞋以外，他出我意料之外地穿了一件白色的長袖襯
衫，一望而知，這件襯衫是全新的。他說他要去當兵
了，穿得如此整整齊齊是為了不讓我看到他的真面目，
我知道他在開玩笑，因為我曾寫過一篇叫做〈真面目〉
的小說。但他的白色長袖襯衫仍然包不住他的黑皮膚，
阿強仍是阿強。

　　阿強又恢復了那種叛逆的表情，一副「不甩」的樣
子，我卻不在乎他的這種態度，畢竟是年輕人，和我幾
乎差了五十歲，這種「不服」的表情，我是看多了，
每次和那些大學部的大學生聊天，他們也都是「不情不
願」的。這些年輕人一定認為和老教授聊天是迫不得已

---

neatly (adv.) 整潔地　　　　　　　attitude (n.) 態度

One day, there was a knock on the door of my study. Opening the door, I saw A-Chiang standing there. This time he was very neatly dressed. Besides wearing jeans and white tennis shoes, much to my surprise, he was wearing a white, long-sleeved shirt. At a glance, I knew it was brand new. He said that he was going to enter military service and was dressed up like this because he didn't want me to see the real him. I knew that he was joking, because I had written a short story called "The Real Me." His long-sleeved shirt however didn't completely cover his dark skin; A-Chiang was still A-Chiang.

A-Chiang quickly returned to his wild expression, a look of "who gives a damn?" But I didn't care about this attitude of his. He was still a young man, who was fifty years younger than me. This "not giving in" I have seen many times. Each time when I talk with undergraduates, they are always most "unwilling." These young people certainly

---

give in 屈服

的事情，必須耍「酷」，才能保持自己的年輕人的尊嚴。

　　阿強除了辭行之外，還送了我一個信封，打開一看，裡面有幾千元，是捐給博幼基金會的，他附了一張紙，上面寫了一句話「大庇天下阿強俱歡顏」。還好我知道這是出典於杜甫的詩，「安得廣廈千萬間，大庇天下寒士俱歡顏」。我謝謝他的時候，眼淚幾乎奪眶而出。這麼一位善良的孩子，就因為家境不好，而無法升學。

---

unavoidable (adj.) 無可避免的　　　　tear (n.) 眼淚
sheet (n.) 一張(紙)　　　　　　　　　stream (v.) 流動

think that talking to their old professor is something that is unavoidable. A young person still must be "cool," however, to maintain his sense of self-respect.

Besides coming to visit me to say good-bye, A-Chiang also wrote me a letter. When I opened it there were a few thousand NT in it, a donation for the Boyo Foundation. There was also one sheet on which was written: "May every 'A-Chiang' in the World be Blessed with a Smiling Face." Fortunately I knew that this was from Tu Fu's poem: "If I could get houses with thousands of rooms, every poor scholar in the world be blessed with a smiling face." When I thanked him, tears were streaming down from my eyes. This very good-natured child was not able to advance to senior high school simply because his family background was not good.

---

good-natured (adj.) 天性善良的　　advance (v.) 前進、晉升

中英對照

　　前天，又收到了阿強的信，他說他看了我寫的新書《一切從基本做起》以後，有些感慨，這些感慨用一句詩可以形容，「萬山不許一溪奔」，這次難倒我了，我不知道這句詩出典何處，但我懂得阿強的意思是什麼。我趕快去問一位中文系教授，他給了我這首詩的全文，「萬山不許一溪奔，攔得溪聲日夜喧，到得前頭山腳盡，堂堂溪水出前村。」我又想起了那位黑皮膚的年輕人，永遠長話短說，永遠長問短答，永遠「不甩」的表情，但是我們是沒有代溝的，我瞭解他，他也瞭解我。

　　　　　　　　　──原載二○○四年八月三日《聯合報》

The day before yesterday, I received another letter from A-Chiang, saying that after he read my new book *Everything Starts from the Basics* he had a feeling which can be described by this line of poetry: "The mountains many let not the stream to flow," This time I was at a loss to know where this line came from, but I understood A-Chiang's meaning. I immediately went to ask a teacher from the Chinese Department about this line and he gave me a copy of the entire poem:

The mountains many let not the stream to flow,
Day and night the blocked stream laments.
Upon reaching the bottom of the mountains,
A river mgnificent appears by the village.

I then thought of that dark-skinned young man, whose words were always few in explanation and answer. He was forever "not giving a damn." But there was no generation gap between us. I understood him and he me.

---

lament (v.) 哀悼　　　　　　magnificent (adj.) 壯麗的

阿傑的姑媽
A-Chieh's Auntie

鮑端磊　譯

　　阿傑的確是個糊塗的孩子，但唯有糊裡糊塗，才能得到心靈上的平安。那些精明到極點的人，要想得到平安，真是比駱駝通過針孔還難。

A-Chieh really is a confused and muddle-headed child. But only the confused and muddle-headed find peace. It is easier for a camel to pass through the eye of a needle than it is for an intelligent and talented man to find peace.

前些日子，我正在和我的研究生阿傑討論功課的時候，他的手機忽然響了，阿傑講了一些話以後，告訴我他的姑媽病危，他必須趕到醫院去。我當然無所謂，他匆匆地走了。

不久以後，阿傑告訴我，他的姑媽已經離開人世了，她信天主教，葬禮也採用天主教儀式。他說他的姑媽孤苦伶仃，無親無戚，他很怕葬禮冷冷清清，所以請我去參加。他的同學也都會去，我一口就答應了他。

事後，我覺得這件事情有點不通，因為阿傑有個大家庭，好多親戚，他的姑媽怎麼會無親無戚？我怎麼也

---

discuss (v.) 討論　　　　　　inform (v.) 通知
assignment (n.) 作業　　　　Catholic (n.) 天主教徒
graduate student 研究生　　funeral ceremony 葬禮
indicate (v.) 指出　　　　　according to 根據

Several days ago, when I was discussing some assignments with my graduate student A-Chieh, his cell phone suddenly rang. After he spoke a bit, A-Chieh told me his auntie was seriously ill, and he had to get to the hospital in a hurry. I of course indicated that was all very fine, and off he quickly went.

Not long after that, A-Chieh informed me that his auntie had left this world of ours. She was a Catholic, and her funeral ceremony was to be according to Catholic ritual. He said his auntie was lonely. She had no relatives at all, and he feared her funeral might be a cold and rather desolate affair. So, he invited me to attend. His classmates were to participate as well. I immediately agreed to be there.

Afterwards, I got to thinking that this all seemed a trifle unusual. A-Chieh came from a large family and had a flock

---

ritual (n.) 儀式
lonely (adj.) 孤獨的
relative (n.) 親戚
participate (v.) 參加

agree (v.) 同意
a trifle 有點
unusual (adj.)不尋常

想不通，最後我直接去找阿傑，問他究竟是怎麼一回事，阿傑支支吾吾地告訴我一個好有趣的故事。

　　阿傑是一個非常粗心大意的人，他只有在做研究的時候才會細心。我不停地發現他忘了鑰匙，或者是丟掉了手機，甚至還會忘記了和女朋友講好的約會。他也是個心地很好的人，媽媽叫他去做的事，他大概都會去做。這次，媽媽給他的任務是要他去探訪他的姑媽，他到了醫院，才發現他根本就不記得他姑媽的名字，好在他記得病房號碼是三十一號病房，所以他就進去了。

relation (n.) 親屬　　　　　　　bother (v.) 費心
hem and haw 支支吾吾　　　　detail (n.) 細節
muddle-headed (adj.) 頭腦不清楚　lose track of 失了線索、下落
in the throes of 辛勞、苦幹

of relatives. How in the world could it be that his auntie didn't have any relations? I couldn't make any sense out of it, and in the end went directly to A-Chieh and asked him just what the score was. Biting his tongue and hemming and hawing, he told me an interesting story.

A-Chieh was a guy who at times could be awfully muddle-headed. Only when he was in the throes of his research did he bother about details. I had always found A-Chieh to be the sort to not know where he had left his keys, or to lose track of his cell phone, or even forget all about a date he'd arranged with his girlfriend. He was also a man with a warm and caring heart. If his mother asked him to go do something, he was very likely to march right off and do it. This time the mission his mother gave him to carry out was to go to the hospital and visit his auntie. When he arrived at the hospital, it dawned on A-Chieh

---

date (n.) 約會
arrange (v.) 安排
warm (adj.) 熱誠、溫暖

mission (n.) 任務
carry out 執行、完成
dawn (v.) 開始明白到

　　三十一號病房的病人是一位老太太，看到阿傑，顯得非常高興。阿傑曾經見過姑媽，但是並不能完全記得她的模樣，在他的心目中，老太太都一個樣子的，所以他和這位老太太有談有笑。老太太把他叫成另一個名字，他也不以為意，他想人老了，總會認錯人的。

　　因為這位姑媽好喜歡和阿傑聊天，阿傑就決定常去看她。每一次老人和年輕人都聊得很快樂，阿傑家住在台中，他每兩週從埔里回台中一次，每次都會去看臥病

---

elderly (adj) 年長的　　　　　　　appear (v.)顯露出、看起來
occupy (v.) 據有、住

that he couldn't quite recall his auntie's name. All he could remember was that her room was number 31. So that was the room he stepped into.

An elderly woman did occupy room number 31. When she saw A-Chieh, she appeared very happy indeed. A-Chieh had seen his auntie in the past, but he was unable to recall with absolute clarity what she looked like. Looking at them from his heart, women up in years all looked pretty much the same to him. So, he talked and laughed with this elderly woman, and when she called him by another name, he didn't think too much about it. He just figured, you know how older folks are. They can never keep straight who is who.

A-Chieh decided to go visit her often because the elderly woman so enjoyed talking with him. The words flew happily back and forth every time this aging woman and young man met. A-Chieh's family lived in Taichung. He

---

clarity (n.) 清晰   visit (v.) 拜訪

的姑媽。姑媽有時會提起他小時候的事情，他一點印象
都沒有，他想這大概是他記性不太好的關係，小時候的
事情已經忘掉了，虧得老姑媽記得。

　　有一天，阿傑去看姑媽的時候，正好一位天主教神
父也在那裡，正在替姑媽祈禱。他這下發現不對了，因
為他們家的宗教信仰都是台灣的民俗宗教，他的姑媽不
可能信天主教的，而且他又忽然想起他姑媽為什麼國語
說得如此之好，他偷偷跑出去查看護理站的資料，才發
現他真正的姑媽的確住在隔壁的隔壁，但早已出院了，

---

childhood (n.) 童年　　　　　　recollection (n.) 記憶、回憶
slight (adj) 一點點、少量

traveled from Puli back to Taichung every two weeks. A-Chieh made it a point to go see that auntie of his in the hospital bed. Every once in a while the auntie would bring up some incident from his childhood. He didn't have the slightest recollection of it, and attributed the problem to his own poor memory. He had forgotten so much from his childhood days. Fortunately, the memory of the elderly auntie was as sharp as could be.

Once when A-Chieh went to see the auntie, a Catholic priest just happened to be there too. He was praying with her. That is when A-Chieh discovered the whole thing was totally wrong. The reason was that his family believed in Taiwanese folk religion. It was impossible for his auntie to be Catholic. Also, it suddenly occurred to him that his auntie spoke Mandarin Chinese remarkably

---

attribute (v.)歸因於   priest (n.)神父

他一直在拜訪的這位老人，不知道是誰的姑媽。

那位神父卻對阿傑讚美有加，告訴他將來必有好
報，而且也要了阿傑的電話號碼，因為老太太沒有什麼
親人了，萬一有事，這位神父會找他來的。這位神父知
道阿傑和老太太都認錯了人，可是他不以為意，他又告
訴阿傑老太太年歲已大，隨時可能離開人世，阿傑必須
心理有所準備。

---

sneak (v.) 偷偷走、溜　　　　pile (v.) 堆、疊
discharge (v.) 准許離開　　　reward (n.) 獎賞

well. He snuck off to the nursing station. That was when A-Chieh discovered his actual auntie had been in the room next door to the room of the elderly woman, and had been discharged some time earlier. All the while, he'd been visiting this elderly woman. He did not know whose auntie she was.

The Catholic priest piled one word of praise after the other on A-Chieh. Said his reward would be great in the future. As a matter of fact, he wrote down A-Chieh's telephone number because the elderly woman didn't have any family to speak of. In the event of anything happening, this priest would give him a call. The priest knew A-Chieh and the elderly woman had mistaken the identity of one another. He did not consider that a problem at all. He also told A-Chieh the elderly woman was quite up in years, and could leave this world at any time really, and so A-Chieh

---

mistake (v.) 誤認   identity (n.) 身分

　　雖然阿傑發現自己認錯了姑媽，他卻仍然照舊地去看這位姑媽，姑媽越來越弱，但每次看到阿傑來，都會露出笑容。臨走以前，她好像在等阿傑，阿傑趕到，她再度露出一種心滿意足的笑容，然後就安詳的過去了。

　　葬禮在一座天主堂裡舉行，小教堂裡擠滿了人，我的學生告訴我都是阿傑的親友。阿傑的爸爸、媽媽、弟弟都坐在第一排，據說，他的舅舅、阿姨、姑媽、姑丈等等來一大堆，他的同學更是傾巢而出。阿傑是台中衛

---

mentally (adv.) 心理上　　　　　rush (v.) 衝去
prepared (adj.) 有所準備的　　　peacefully (adv.) 平靜地
beam (v.) 展露笑容　　　　　　conduct (v.) 引導、引領

had better get mentally prepared for the loss.

Although A-Chieh discovered he had made this mistake, he kept up his visits with her. The auntie was getting weaker by the day, but every time her eyes lit upon A-Chieh, the smile on her face just beamed. When the end came, it appeared she was waiting for A-Chieh. He rushed to her side, the smile on her face said she was satisfied, and she peacefully slipped away.

The funeral was conducted at a Catholic church. The little church was jammed with people. My students said they were all members of the A-Chieh family. A-Chieh's father and mother sat in the first pew. His maternal uncle, his maternal aunt and assorted uncles and aunts were all there as a group. A-Chieh's classmates were there en masse. A-Chieh had graduated from Viator High

---

church (n.) 教堂
jam (v.) 擠滿
pew (n.) 教堂座位

maternal (adj.) 母系的
en masse 全體
graduate (v.) 畢業

道中學畢業的，所以會唱聖歌，他的碩士班同學在他的指揮之下，從頭唱到尾，「上主，求你垂憐」，還是用希臘文唱的。主禮神父講道講得很短，他引用了我寫的〈陌生人〉作為主軸，強調替陌生人服務是件好事，滑稽的是這位神父說這個故事雖好，但他不記得這是誰寫的，他還畫蛇添足地說，這一定是一位不有名的作家寫的，否則他一定記得。我就坐在下面，聽了人家說我是位不有名的作家，只有苦笑的分。

彌撒的福音用的是真福八端，這位神父還加了一

hymn (n.) 聖歌　　　　　　preach (v.) 宣講、講道
service (n.) 儀式　　　　　　sermon (n.) 佈道

School in Taichung, and he knew many hymns. He led his classmates from graduate school like a glee club instructor, and they sang the whole service through from start to finish. That even included the Greek "Kyrie," the "Lord, have mercy on me." The priest who led the ceremony preached a short sermon. He actually based his remarks on a piece I myself had written called "The Stranger." He emphasized that service for a stranger was a noble act. There was a touch of the comic there as well. The priest said that although the story was a good one, he could not remember the name of the author. He then put his foot into his mouth by adding that the author couldn't have been very famous because otherwise he'd surely have recalled his name. There I was sitting right in front of him and hearing him say I wasn't a writer anyone would know. I smiled wryly.

The Bible text for the gospel was the Sermon on the

---

remark (n.) 言論、評論
emphasize (v.) 強調

noble (adj.) 高貴的
touch (n.) 一點點、少許

句，「糊裡糊塗的人是有福的，因為他們必定得到心靈中的平安。」

在起靈以前，阿傑獨唱〈我有平安如江河〉，我只知道阿傑喜歡唱歌，沒有想到他唱得如此好聽。唱完以後，他的好友們將棺木抬上靈車，靈車啟動之前，阿傑在教堂門口向全體送葬的親友鞠躬。至少對我而言，他完全變了一個人，阿傑永遠是個嘻嘻哈哈的人，可是現在變得一臉嚴肅的表情，一位同學送他去火葬場，那位同學說阿傑在車裡淚流滿面。

葬禮結束了，阿傑忙著做研究，他的研究做得有聲

---

virtue (n.) 美德　　　　　　casket (n.) 棺材
without a doubt 無疑　　　　hearse (n.) 靈車
imagine (v.) 想像　　　　　congregation (n.) 會眾

Mount, sometimes called the Eight Great Virtues. The priest added a line. "Blessed are the confused and muddleheaded, for without a doubt peace will descend upon their hearts."

Before the final blessing, A-Chieh sang as a solo the hymn "I've got Peace Like the River Jordan." I always knew he liked to sing, but I never imagined he could sing so beautifully. After the hymn he and his friends carried the casket out to the hearse. A-Chieh led the congregation at the door of the church in bows of respect for the deceased. In my eyes, he had become a whole new person. A-Chieh had always been a smiling, happy go-lucky fellow. Now however he wore a serious expression upon his face. A classmate of his accompanied him to the crematorium. He said A-Chieh wept inside the car.

After the funeral, A-Chieh busied himself with his

---

respect (n.) 尊敬
decease (v.) 死亡

crematorium (n.) 火葬場
weep (v.) 哭泣

有色，非常令人滿意。每一位老師都說他聰明。他究竟是聰明，還是糊塗呢？預官報名時，阿傑忘得一乾二淨，這下，也沒有服國防役的可能了。別人碰到這種事情，會懊惱不已，阿傑只沮喪了一下子，馬上就忘了這件事情，他說當大頭兵，有什麼了不起。看到阿傑這種模樣，我想起了他的獨唱〈我有平安如江河〉。

阿傑的確是個糊塗的孩子，但唯有糊裡糊塗，才能得到心靈上的平安。那些精明到極點的人，要想得到平安，真是比駱駝通過針孔還難。難怪那位神父不記得我的名字了。

——原載二〇〇五年三月二十八日《聯合報》

---

excellent（adj.）優秀的　　　　accomplishment（n.）成就

research, which was truly excellent. Everyone expressed satisfaction with his accomplishment. Every professor said he was so intelligent. Was A-Chieh, however, intelligent, or was he muddle-headed? He completely forgot he was qualified for officer training and missed filing the proper paper work. He therefore was not even registered for his military reserve duty. If someone else had done that, he'd likely have lost his mind. But A-Chieh? Well, he did feel very down in the dumps about it for a while, but he soon forgot all about it. What was the big deal about being a hot shot lieutenant, anyway? When I saw A-Chieh like that, I thought of his singing that hymn, "I've got Peace Like the River Jordan."

A-Chieh really is a confused and muddle-headed child. But only the confused and muddle-headed find peace. It is easier for a camel to pass through the eye of a needle than it is for an intelligent and talented man to find peace. No wonder that Catholic priest couldn't remember my name.

---

qualified (adj.) 合乎資格的   file (v.) 提出、提交

A、B、C錶
My Watches "A", "B", and "C"

康士林　譯

　　這三支錶事實上沒有造成我任何損失，它們究竟要送什麼訊息給我呢？

Actually these three watches never cost me anything. But what was the message that they wanted to give me?

最近，我看了一部影集，偵探是Mr. Monk。大偵探看了現場以後，發現現場的鐘快了幾小時之久，這成了大偵探破案的重要線索。電影裡的殺人凶器是磁鐵，磁鐵出現，鐘的時針和分針都會大亂，當時我就有點緊張，因為我和磁鐵似乎有點關係。

話說我過去一直用一支錶，我們可以將它稱之為A錶，這支錶一直走得很好。但大約一年以前，它會忽然慢一小時左右。比方說，現在是六時二十分，而這支錶是五時十五分。但奇怪的是它雖然慢了一小時，現在又走得完全正常。

---

television series 電視影集　　　weapon (n.) 武器
detective (n.) 偵探　　　　　　murder (n.) 兇手
scene (n.) 場景　　　　　　　　magnet (n.) 磁石、磁鐵
clue (n.) 線索

Recently I was watching a television series; the detective was Mr. Monk. After this great detective saw the scene of the crime, he discovered that the clock there was fast by a few hours, which became the clue for the great detective to break the case. The weapon used by the murderer in the film was a magnet; and with the appearance of the magnet, the clock's hour and minute hands went wacky. At that time, I became a bit tense, because I seem to have a little relationship with magnets.

Here's the story. In the past I always wore a watch, which we can call my "A" watch. This watch had always been fine. But about a year ago, it became slow by about an hour. When the time is 6:20, my watch says it's 5:15. But the strange thing is that even though it is slow by an hour, it still operates completely normally.

---

appearance (n.) 出現
wacky (adj.) 古怪的、發瘋的
tense (adj.) 緊繃的、緊張的

relationship (n.) 關係
operate (v.) 運作
normally (adv.) 正常地

　　有一次，我和我的學生陳奎昊開車到埔里去，出發的時候，我看了一下錶，是七時十分。奎昊也看到我看錶的，而且也聽到我念七時十分。一個多小時以後，我們到達草屯的一家萊爾富便利商店吃早餐，我又看了我的錶，令我大吃一驚的是，我的錶指在七點二十分，好像從新竹到草屯，只開了十分鐘。正確的時間是八點半左右，我的錶慢了一小時十分鐘。這次，奎昊看到了。由於開車離開新竹的時候，我的錶是正確的，在車上的一個半小時內，難道我的錶停了整整一小時十分鐘，然後又恢復正常走動？當然還有一個可能，那就是我的錶的時針自動撥回了一小時十分鐘。兩者都是不可思議的。

---

convenience store 便利商店　　　　exactly (adv.) 正好、恰好
correct (adj.) 正確的　　　　　　　accurately (adv.) 準確地

One time, I drove to Puli with my student Chen Kuei-hao; as we were starting out, I took a look at my watch, which said 7:10. Kuei-hao also saw my watch and heard me say 7:10. After over an hour, we stopped at a Hi-Light convenience store in Tsaotun for breakfast. I took another look at my watch, and much to my surprise the time my watch indicated was 7:20, as if going from Hsinchu to Tsaotun we had only been on the road for ten minutes. Actually the correct time was about 8:30; my watch was slow an hour and ten minutes. This time, Kuei-hao saw the watch too. Since my watch was correct when we had left Hsinchu and since we were on the road for under an hour and a half, how could it be that my watch stopped exactly for an hour and ten minutes and then started to tick again accurately? There was of course another possibility, which was that my watch's hour hand had automatically turned itself back an hour and ten minutes. But both possibilities

---

possibility (n.) 可能性   automatically (adv.) 自動地

　　我的太太提醒我還有一支錶，我們稱它為B錶吧，B錶是我女兒送的，錶面全黑，分針白色，時針一半紅，一半黑。必須仔細看，否則只看到了分針，看不到時針。有一天，我去高鐵車站搭七點半的車子，到了車站，看了一下錶，只看到了分針指在四十五分，把我嚇出一身冷汗，以為我遲到了。再仔細看時針，發現時針指在六時。當時正確的時間是七點二十分，B錶慢了四十五分鐘。

　　B錶以後慢了好幾次，每次都是一小時左右。不論A錶或B錶，慢了一小時以後，走動完全正常。這種情

---

convincing (adj.) 有說服力的　　　　point (v.) 指著、指向

were not at all convincing.

My wife reminded me that I still had another watch. Let's call it my "B" watch, which was given to me by my daughter. The face of the watch was entirely black and the minute hand was white, with the hour hand being half red and half black. You had to look carefully or you would only see the minute hand and not the hour one. One day, I went to the HSR station to take the 7:30 train. When I arrived at the station and looked at my watch, I only saw the minute hand pointing to 45. I was frightened into a cold sweat, thinking that I had arrived late. When I carefully took another look, I saw that the hour hand was at six. Actually, the correct time was 7:20 and my "B" watch was slow by 45 minutes.

Afterward, my "B" watch was slow on a number of occasions, and each time it was slow by about an hour.

---

frighten (v.) 使⋯⋯害怕   occasion (n.) 場合

況，好像有人將錶的時針撥回五格。

　　有一天，好心的陳奎昊將我的A錶送到了一家在埔里的錶店檢查，店主問我有沒有睡磁性枕頭，我當然沒有。店主修了一下。我有一天在家裡發現這個錶完全停了，只好放棄這支A錶。我太太和我去大遠百買了一支Swatch錶，價值三千元台幣，是我有生以來買的最貴的錶。這是兩星期以前的事。我將此錶稱為C錶。

　　A錶一直放在我的書桌上，五天以前，我太太發現A錶並未停，而是那撥時針的錶冠被拉出來了。我太太

---

intension (n.) 意圖　　　　　　　manager (n.) 經理、負責人

Whether it was my "A" watch or my "B" watch that was slow for an hour, afterwards it operated completely normally. Under these circumstances, it seemed as if someone had pushed my hour hand back by five degrees.

One day, with every good intention, Chen Kuei-hao took my "A" watch to a watch shop in Puli to be checked. The manager asked if I slept on a magnetic pillow, which I of course did not. The manager repaired the watch. Then, one day at home, I discovered that this watch stopped completely, so I had to give up my "A" watch. My wife and I went to FE'21 department store and bought a Swatch watch for 3000 NT. It was the most expensive watch I had ever purchased. This happened two weeks ago. I call this watch my "C" watch.

My "A" watch is always placed on my desk. Five days ago, my wife found that it has indeed not stopped but the

---

give up 放棄   purchase (v.) 購買

一口咬定是我這個糊塗老頭幹的好事，我有口莫辯。我怎麼會去做這種事？我太太將那支錶的錶冠恢復原狀，它就走得好好的。我立刻又戴它，因為我對它有點感情。一天以後，它又慢了半小時。我只好去戴C錶。C錶是全新的，絕不會出問題了。

今天（2008/8/6）早上七時十分，我發現我的C錶快了一小時十分鐘。這件事，陳奎昊可以作證。他親眼看到的。

事已至此，我只好認了。C錶是支新錶，也會作怪，我想我再也不買錶了。

---

button (n.) 按鈕
insist (v.) 堅持
attempt (n.) 嘗試

defense (n.) 辯護、防禦
witness (n.) 證人

button for setting the hour hand had been pulled out. My wife insisted that it was me, a confused, old man, who had done this. How could I do this? My wife push the button back and it started working again. I made no attempt to come to my defense and immediately started to wear it, because I have some feelings for it. One day later, it was again slow by half an hour. I had to change back to my "C" watch, which was all new and certainly would not have any problem.

Today (August 6, 2008) at 7:10 am I discovered that my "C" watch was fast by an hour and ten minutes. Here Chen Kuei-hao can be my witness, for he saw it in person.

With the matter coming to this stage, I could only put up with it. My new "C" also was out of kilter. I decided never to buy another watch.

---

in person 親身、親自　　　　　put up with 忍受
stage (n.) 時期、階段　　　　out of kilter 狀況不佳

　　我的學生們知道我的C錶快了一小時十分鐘，議論紛紛。他們一致問我最近有沒有戴過B錶，我承認我已有好一陣子沒有戴B錶了，他們乘勝追擊，問我B錶有沒有出過問題，我又只好承認我每天都去檢查B錶，它一點問題也沒有。這些同學都不再問，因為事實證明，只要我不去戴它，它就好好的。

　　我的寶貝高足吳柏宏首先對此事表示意見，他用電子郵件向我說：「老師，你向來很有磁性，當然會出這種事情。」我在靜宜大學的高足黃其思也如此說：「老師，你年輕的時候，沒有出過這種事情。老了以後，才

---

prove (v.) 證明、證實　　　　　opinion (n.) 意見

There was much discussion among my students when they knew that my "C" watch was fast by an hour and ten minutes. They were asking me if I had worn my "B" watch recently. I admitted that I had not worn my "B" watch for some time. They kept on questioning me and asked if there had been any problem with my "B" watch. I had to admit that whenever I checked my "B" watch each day, there was no problem with it at all. These students then didn't ask anything else, because the fact was proven: if I didn't wear the watch, it was just fine.

My prized student Wu Po-hung was the first one to express his opinion on this matter. He told me by e-mail: "Professor Li, you have always been very magnetic, so it is no surprise that you should have this problem." Another of my prized students, Huang Chi-tzu at Providence University, said this: "Professor Li, you had no trouble like this when you were young. Since it was only after you

---

magnetic (adj.) 帶磁性的；具吸
引力的

有這種事情，可見有些人，越老越有磁性。」我還有一位綽號叫做「歐弟」的學生，他的意見更有趣了，他說：「老師，以後你戴錶以後，就不要講話，因為你的聲音太有磁性。」

我已七十歲，人老了，就喜歡聽這類令人飄飄然的話。說實話，我真的不知道我的三支錶為何行為如此怪異，但我今天卻開始有點相信，也許我真的有些磁性。我常常想，為何B錶最近一切正常？還不是因為我沒有去戴它的原因。

有一件事是我一直感到困惑的，那就是為什麼三支錶都會慢或快一小時左右。如果它們要整我，可以只差

---

nickname (n.) 暱稱　　　　　　smug (adj.) 沾沾自喜的

were older when you had this problem, it is obvious that some people become more magnetic as they get older." I also had a student whose nickname was O-di. His opinion was even more interesting. He said, "Professor Li, when you wear a watch, you should not talk because your voice is too magnetic."

I'm old, and am already 70. I like to hear words that make me feel smug. To tell the truth, I really didn't know why my three watches were acting so strangely. But I'm now starting to have a little assurance that probably I am a bit magnetic. I was often thinking as to why my "B" watch recently was normal? As it turned out, it was all because I had not been wearing it.

One thing has troubled me however. Why was it that all three watches were slow or fast about one hour? If they wanted to give me a hard time, a difference of ten minutes

---

assurance (n.) 把握、信心

十分鐘，那我根本不會發現。我上課可能遲到，火車可能趕不上。它們差了一小時，我一定會發現。這三支錶事實上沒有造成我任何損失，它們究竟要送什麼訊息給我呢？

　　C錶的時針忽然快一小時，使我更加感到「我的時間不多了」。一定有人在提醒我，我該多多利用寶貴的時間，做一些有意義的事。我已看準了幾個小孩子，打算要教他們英文和數學，我可以想像到他們未來的一臉苦相。我相信，只要我認真地教小孩子，我的三支錶就都會正常了。

——原載二〇〇八年九月二日《聯合報》

would have done it, and I wouldn't have discovered it. Perhaps I would have been late for class or missed my train. But they all had an hour's difference, which I certainly would discover. Actually these three watches never cost me anything. But what was the message that they wanted to give me?

That my "C" watch was suddenly fast by an hour made me feel all the more that "I don't have much time left." Someone was definitely reminding me that I should use my precious time well and do some meaningful things. I had already been certain about some children to whom I should teach English and mathematics. I can already imagine their faces twisting bitterly then. I believed that I only need to go seriously teaching those children and my three watches would be normal.

---

message (n.) 訊息　　　　　　　precious (adj.) 珍貴的

恍神
Absentminded

鮑端磊　譯

　　老張回想起來，每次他有得意的事情，就會聽到「你帶我走」，難怪他領獎的時候會恍神。

　　Old Chang recalled that every time he came upon a moment of unusual success, he would hear "You, take me with you." No wonder then that when he received an award, that spell of confusion and absentmindedness fell upon him.

我們每個人都有過恍神的經驗，有的時候我們在想一個問題，別人和我們說話，我們會完全聽不見。不過這種情況應該是不常發生的。

　　老張卻是一位經常恍神的人。我和他在初中時就是同班同學，他功課很好，老是領獎。每次在台上領獎，就會有兩秒鐘有一種茫然而且困惑的表情。因為這種表情呈現的時間極短，大家雖然注意到了，也沒有人去問他究竟是怎麼一回事。

　　書念完了，老張做了大學教授，我們大家都知道做

---

absentminded (adj.) 心不在焉　　　award (n.) 獎
rank (v.) 排名　　　　　　　　　　fleeting (adj.) 短暫的

All of us have our experiences with being absentminded. Sometimes we may be thinking of a problem, and someone says something to us and we don't catch a word of it. This kind of thing however shouldn't happen very often.

Old Chang though is Mr. Absentminded himself. We were in the same class in high school. Old Chang was really good in academics, and always ranked at the top of the class. Whenever he was on stage to pick up his awards, for about two fleeting seconds a look of bewilderment - - as if he'd forgotten where he was - - would flash across his face. Everyone noticed this, but because this expression came and went so quickly, well, no one actually ever asked him what it was all about.

After he finished his studies, Old Chang became a

---

bewilderment (n.) 困惑   notice (v.) 注意、察覺到
flash (v.) 掠過

教授不容易，要教書，又要做研究。可是老張卻沒有什麼多大的問題，他給我們的感覺是他有點運氣特別好，小的時候就聰明，念書沒有什麼困難。沒有想到的是，他做研究也沒有什麼問題，他很快地升到了正教授，又得到了好多的獎。

我們老朋友經常聚會，發現老張的老毛病沒有減輕。有一天，我們中間的一位實在忍不住了，直接了當地問他為什麼會恍神，在恍神的那一剎那，他究竟在想

---

lucky (adj.) 幸運的
promotion (n.) 升遷、升等
full professor 正教授

accolade (n.) 讚美
frequent (adj.) 經常發生的
occurrence (n.) 事情、事件

university professor. We all know being a professor is not easy. You have the teaching to handle, and then the research too. None of it was much of a problem for Old Chang. The feeling he gave us was that he was an especially lucky fellow. He was smart when he was young, and studying just wasn't at all difficult. What we never thought was that his research didn't give him any problems either. He sailed quickly through the promotion process and soon was a full professor. Accolades and awards just kept right on coming.

Whenever we old friends got together with him, a frequent occurrence, we noticed that Old Chang's weakness hadn't gotten any less. One day, someone in our group just couldn't take it any longer, and blurted the question straight out. He asked Old Chang what this sudden state of discombobulation was all about. When he abruptly

---

weakness (n.) 毛病、缺點　　　discombobulation (n.) 混亂
blurt (v.) 脫口而出　　　　　　abruptly (adv.) 突然地
state (n.) 狀態

什麼？他說他其實什麼也沒有想，只是他會無緣無故地聽到一個聲音，說「你帶我走」。對老張來講，這句話毫無意義，因此他免不了會想一下這是怎麼一回事，因為得不到答案，也就算了。他沒有想到他從初中開始聽到這個聲音，現在已是中年，仍然會聽到這個聲音。

我們大家都代他擔心，因為我們都想到一部叫作《美麗境界》的電影，電影中的男主角納許是諾貝爾獎

---

consciousness (n.) 意識　　　　　affair (n.) 事件、事情
without rhyme or reason 沒道
理、莫名其妙

lost consciousness of where he was and what he was doing, what was happening inside his head, anyway? He answered that, actually, nothing at all was on his mind when it happened.

The only thing was, without rhyme or reason, he'd hear a voice say "You, take me with you!" As far as Old Chang was concerned, the words made no sense. Thus he couldn't help but think the whole affair was just very odd. He of course gave some thought to it, but could never get an answer for it, and simply left it at that. It never occurred to him that at middle life he would still be hearing the voice he'd heard in high school.

We were all quite concerned because a movie came to our mind called *A Beautiful Mind* The protagonist in the film was John Forbes Nash, Jr., the Nobel Laureate in

---

protagonist (n.) 主角   film (n.) 電影

得主，極為聰明，但有幻聽的病，常會聽到莫須有的聲音。有一位老朋友因此建議老張去看看這方面的醫生。老張說他早就去看過了，但他們一致認定他沒有病。他們說幻聽的人不可能永遠聽到同一句話的。

又有一位朋友問他，是小孩還是成人的聲音？老張想了一下，說這是孩子的聲音。那位朋友問他是男孩還是女孩，他說男女都有。

我們又問他在什麼情況之下會聽到這個聲音，他說

exceptionally (adv.) 特別地   illness (n.) 疾病
intelligent (adj.) 聰明   murmur (v.) 低聲說話
hallucinatory (adj.) 幻覺的   specialize (v.) 專精

Economics, who is exceptionally intelligent, but suffers from hallucinatory hearing, an illness that causes him to hear voices murmuring in his ear. A buddy suggested to Old Chang that he consult a doctor that specializes in this condition. Old Chang said he had already gone to doctors. They had all confirmed that nothing was wrong with his health. They claimed it could not happen that a person with hallucinatory hearing would hear the same words all the time.

When someone asked if it were the voice of a child or an adult, Old Chang thought a moment and said it was the voice of a child. The friend asked if the voice were of a girl or a boy, and he said he had heard both.

We also asked him the nature of the circumstances in which he heard this voice. His answer was that he had

---

condition (n.) 狀態、症狀
confirm (v.) 證實、確認
claim (v.) 聲稱

nature (n.) 性質
circumstance (n.) 情況、狀況

他曾經做了一下統計，發現在各種場合都會有，他領獎的時候，幾乎一定會聽到這種聲音。他看報、瀏覽網站或者看電視的時候，也會聽到。至於什麼節目，或者什麼新聞，他記不太清楚。可是他回想起來，他看BBC網站新聞或者是BBC電視新聞的時候，往往會聽到。

老張幻聽的情形，使得他太太有點害怕，她一直相信老張太喜歡做研究，所以常和老張開車到鄉下去玩。週末鄉下人不多，老張有時看到一所小學，就進去走走，他作夢也沒有想到，在這種偏僻的鄉下，他更會聽到「你帶我走」。

---

sort (n.) 種類　　　　　　program (n.) 電視節目
surf the Internet 上網　　report (n.) 報導、報告
occur (v.) 發生

once taken notes and discovered he could hear it in many sorts of places. Whenever he received an award, he was sure to hear the voice. When he read a newspaper or surfed the Internet or watched television he could also hear it. He did not remember everything so clearly, whether it occurred with certain programs or during certain kinds of news reports. He recalled, however, hearing it when he read BBC News online or watched BBC News on television.

Old Chang's hearing of these imaginary voices made his wife feel a bit scared. She always felt Old Chang loved his research just a little too much. So she often drove with him to relax in the countryside. On weekends there weren't many folks around. Old Chang would see an elementary school and step inside for a look around. He would suddenly get dreamy and who would have thought that in

---

imaginary (adj.) 想像的、幻想的　　relax (v.) 放鬆
scared (adj.) 害怕的、恐懼的　　countryside (n.) 鄉間

　　我們問他在什麼時候，他一定不會聽到。這點他也可以回答，他說他和家人親友在一起的時候，好像從未聽過，打網球的時候，從未聽過，做研究的時候，從未聽過，看偵探小說的時候，從未聽過。但是主日望彌撒的時候，會聽見，而且常常聽見。

　　我們都想不通這是怎麼一回事，但大家也不太擔心老張，因為他顯然知道他自己幻聽，而且他的幻聽似乎沒有對他有任何影響。

---

distant (adj.) 遙遠的

desolated (adj.) 荒蕪的

definitely (adv.) 明確地

tennis (n.) 網球

such a distant and desolated place he'd still hear the words "You, take me with you"?

We asked when this definitely did not happen to him. He had an answer for this. He said whenever he was with his family or friends, it seemed he never heard the voices. Playing tennis, he never heard anything. Doing research, he never heard anything. Reading a crime story, he never heard anything. But when he was at Mass on Sundays, he could hear the voice. In fact, it often happened there.

None of us could figure any of this out, but no one was overly concerned about Old Chang. It was clear that he himself knew that he had hallucinatory hearing. What was more, the problem did not affect him in any negative way.

---

crime (n.) 罪行、犯罪　　　affect (v.) 影響
overly (adv.) 過度地　　　　negative (adj.) 負面的

　　前些日子，我們大家到郊外去爬山，到了山腰，要走一段石階，才可以走到山頂。在山腰，我們看到了一個小男孩站在石階的起步地方，他走了一下，就停了下來，從他走路的姿勢來看，他是殘障的，雖能走路，但是一個跛子，他走路的樣子實在很可憐，看來他很想上山，但大概是上不去了。老張二話不說，問他要不要由他扶他上去，小男孩點點頭，於是老張和小男孩打頭陣，我們都慢慢地爬上了山頂。山頂有一個可以休息的地方，老張安排小男孩坐下，讓他可以看到山下的美景。小男孩笑得好高興，也一再地謝謝老張。

---

mountain climbing 爬山　　　　posture (n.) 姿態
recently (adv.) 最近　　　　　　ascertain (v.) 確定
suburb (n.) 郊區　　　　　　　physically challenged 肢體障礙
flight (n.) 一階、一段　　　　　lame (adj.) 跛腳的

A group of us went mountain climbing recently in the suburbs. We reached half way up the mountain and then came upon a flight of stone steps, which was the only way that led to the top. Half way up that mountain we saw a little boy who stood at the foot of the steps. He took a step forward and then stopped. From his posture we ascertained that he was physically challenged. He was able to walk all right, but he was lame. His way of walking was truly pitiful. It looked like he had his heart set on climbing that mountain, but there was probably just no way he could do it. Old Chang went right up to him. He asked the boy if he wanted him to help him make the ascent. The little fellow nodded his head. Old Chang and the little boy lead the attack as we made our way slowly up to the peak. There was a rest area at the top of the mountain, and Old Chang helped the boy sit in a way that could look out and take in all that wonderful scenery below. The little boy laughed

---

pitiful (adj.) 令人生憐的
probably (adv.) 或許
ascent (n.) 上升、上坡

nod (v.) 點(頭)
peak (n.) 山頂
scenery (n.) 風景

　　我們要下山了，老張問小男孩要不要和我們一起下去，因為上山容易下山難，如果小男孩沒有人攙扶，是一定下不了山的。但是出乎我們意料之外的是，小男孩搖搖頭，說他還想看風景。

　　我們發現小男孩好像很堅決，只好自己下山了。到了山下，老張忽然問我們小男孩是否穿短褲，我們不約而同說他穿的是短褲。他又問，殘障的小孩會喜歡短褲嗎？這的確問倒了我們。然後，老張又問我們一個問題，孩子的腿是不是很粗壯？我們回想起來，結論是孩

---

descend (v.) 下去、下降　　　　steep (adj.) 陡峭
descent (n.) 下坡　　　　　　　unexpectedly (adv.) 出乎意料地

happily and kept thanking Old Chang.

When it was time for us to descend the mountain, Old Chang asked the boy if he wanted to go with us. Climbing down is harder than climbing up, and the descent was so steep that if he didn't have a little help, there was just no way he'd be able to do it. Unexpectedly, however, the boy shook his head and said he wanted to stay up there and enjoy the scenery.

We found the little boy was quite determined indeed, so we headed down by ourselves. When we arrived at the foot of the mountain, Old Chang suddenly asked us if the little boy was wearing shorts. We all said he had been wearing shorts. Old Chang asked us, "Does a little guy who is physically impaired like to wear shorts?" After that Old Chang asked something else. "Were the legs of the child

---

enjoy (v.) 享受、欣賞　　　　　impaired (adj.) 受損的
determined (adj.) 堅定、下定決
心的

子的兩條腿又黑又粗壯，難怪他不要我們幫他下山。

　　但小男孩為什麼要騙我們呢？在路上，我們都在想這個問題，誰也沒有得到答案。到了晚上，我已上床睡覺，老張打電話給我，說他知道這是怎麼一回事了，而且他認為他以後再也不會恍神了。我當時睡意正濃，懶得聽他解釋，他也沒有解釋。

　　從此以後，老張不再恍神了。他也常常約不到，為

---

trick (v.) 捉弄、欺騙　　　　ponder (v.) 思索、沉思
perplex (v.) 使……困惑　　　asleep (adj.) 睡著了的

very strong?" We thought back on it and recalled the boy's legs were dark and strong. No wonder he didn't want our help getting down the mountain.

But why would the little boy want to trick us? The question perplexed us. We pondered this on our way back. No one could come up with an answer. That night I was already asleep in bed when Old Chang called me on the telephone. He said he had come to an understanding about the whole thing. Not only that, but he thought that from that time onward, he wouldn't be having any of those absent-minded spells of his. I had been in the midst of a very deep sleep, and was by no means keen on listening to his explanation. Anyway, he really didn't explain anything.

From that moment on, Old Chang no longer got discombobulated. He frequently excused himself from our

---

keen (adj.) 熱切的   explain (v.) 解釋
explanation (n.) 解釋

什麼呢？他從那天起，就開始教一些弱勢孩子的英文和
數學。有一天，有一位富翁捐了一筆錢給他，他就一不
做、二不休，成立了一個基金會，大規模地幫助弱勢的
孩子。

　　老張告訴我們，他要開始走石階的時候，又聽到了
「你帶我走」，他終於瞭解了這句話的含義，他雖然一
帆風順地在社會上越爬越高，但很多可憐的孩子其實是
不可能像他一樣地往上爬的。因此他們向他求助，希望
他能帶他們也往上爬，但他始終聽不懂。直到那一天，
在山腰看到那位小男孩，他終於搞懂了「你帶我走」是
什麼意思。

---

disabled (adj.) 肢障的　　　　donation (n.) 捐款
wealthy (adj.) 有錢的　　　　　idle (adj.) 閒置的
hefty (adj.) 大量的

get-togethers. Why? It turned out that from that day on, he began giving English and mathematics lessons to disabled children. Then one day a very wealthy man made a hefty donation. Old Chang didn't leave it idle. He used it to establish a carefully constructed foundation for the care of children with disabilities.

Old Chang told us that when he was about to start climbing the stone steps on the mountainside, and again heard the words "You, take me with you," he finally understood what the words meant. Although he himself had been sailing along and moving smoothly up the ladder of society, there was many a poor child who could never make that climb like him. So they called out for him to help them. They hoped he could help them make that climb too. He had always heard the words, but never grasped their meaning. Until that day, that is, when he saw

---

establish (v.) 設立
foundation (n.) 基金會

ladder (n.) 梯子、階梯
grasp (v.) 理解

　　老張回想起來，每次他有得意的事情，就會聽到「你帶我走」，難怪他領獎的時候會恍神。除此以外，當他看到人類悲慘的新聞的時候，也會聽到。顯然有人在提醒他，不要自顧自的，也要幫助那些沒有他那麼幸運的人。

　　老張有一個小孩，小時常有數學的問題，每次老張都會替他解惑，上國中的時候，一開始英文有點困難，也是由老張夫婦指點一下，以後就沒有問題。老張還請

---

success (n.) 成功　　　　　　　particularly (adv.) 特別地

the little boy on the side of the mountain. Then it sank in, what this "You, take me with you" meant.

Old Chang recalled that every time he came upon a moment of unusual success, he would hear "You, take me with you." No wonder then that when he received an award, that spell of confusion and absentmindedness fell upon him. In addition to those moments, whenever he learned of particularly tragic news events, the words came back to him again. Clearly someone out there kept reminding him that he should not simply go about his own business, but help people who were not as lucky as he was.

Old Chang had a child who had trouble with mathematics. Old Chang solved his problems every time. When he was in high school, the child had difficulties at first with English, and again it was Old Chang that came to his assistance. Afterwards there were no problems. What was more, Old

---

tragic (adj.) 悲劇的、悲慘的　　　assistance (n.) 協助

了一位他的博士班學生做他兒子的家教，所以他的兒子念書很順利。

不僅此也，老張的兒子從小就有看書的習慣，老張夫婦常常出國旅行，兒子從小就知道一大堆別的孩子不知道的事情，現在兒子念很好的國立高中，已經學會了寫程式，可以看英文小說。老張並沒有把握他兒子一定會非常傑出，可是要在社會上爬上上層階級，一定是毫無問題的。

老張知道很多孩子沒有如此幸運，他們的父親沒有辦法教他們英文和數學，也沒有錢替他們請家教，更沒有錢送他們去補習班；他們不要說到國外去旅遊了，恐怕連島內很多地方都沒有去過；看書的習慣更加是沒有

tutor (v.) 輔導　　　　　habit (n.) 習慣

Chang asked one of his doctoral students to tutor his child at home, so his son sailed through academically.

Not only that, but Old Chang's son developed a habit for studying from early on. Old Chang and his wife traveled abroad frequently, and their son knew a lot of things that other children didn't know. Their son presently studies at a very good public high school and is good at writing computer programs and can read English novels. Old Chang is not certain that his son will shine, but it's clear the child is on a straight path to success up the steps of society.

Old Chang knows that many children are not this lucky. Their dads have no way to teach them English or mathematics, and haven't enough money to hire someone for home-tutoring, much less send them to a cram school. These children have not seen much of the island,

---

presently (adj.) 目前   hire (v.) 聘用

的。這種弱勢的孩子，要想在社會上往上爬，當然很困難。

老張下定決心，儘量地幫助一些弱勢孩子補習。他發現他的確是幫得上忙的，給他教過的孩子，功課都好很多。他所成立的基金會幫助的孩子就更多了，而最重要的是，他再也沒有聽到「你帶我走」的聲音。

前天，我去老張的基金會參觀，令我感到十分有趣的是一幅畫，畫中有一位成年人牽著一個小孩的手，走上石階，畫的下面寫了「我帶你走」四個字。老張曾經

---

not to mention 更別提　　　　equally (adv.) 相等地、相同地

not to mention traveled abroad. A habit of studying is equally unthinkable for them. For children with disabilities it is of course just very hard to even think about climbing higher in life.

Old Chang is absolutely determined to do the best he can to help these children study well. He has discovered that he indeed could be of help. The children he has taught have all done well. Many more have received help from his foundation. Most important of all, he no longer hears that voice that says, "You, take me with you."

The day before yesterday, I went to Old Chang's foundation to take a look around. I found an interesting painting there. An adult holds the hand of a child. A group of middle-aged people is climbing a flight of steps. At the bottom of the painting are four words: "You, take me with

---

painting (n.) 畫作

將很多菁英分子帶到了社會的高層，看來，他不以此為
滿足，他要將很多弱勢的孩子推到社會較高的階層去。

——原載二〇〇八年十二月二十四日《聯合報》

you." The three words "You, carry me" are written on the canvas. Old Chang has carried many bright children up the long flight of steps of society. I can see, however, that he is not satisfied yet. He wants to push children with disabilities up even higher steps.

---

canvas (n.) 畫布　　　　　　　satisfied (adj.) 滿意的

譯者簡介

康士林（Nicholas Koss）

美國印第安那大學比較文學博士，現任天主教輔仁大學比較文學研究所專任教授。自一九八一年起於輔仁大學英國文學系任教迄今。康教授並於輔仁大學比較文學研究所與翻譯學研究所授課。最近剛卸下六年任期的外語學院院長行政職。康教授著有專書：*The Best and Fairest Land: Medieval Images of China*，數篇比較文學相關學術論文及台灣*The Chinese Pen* 翻譯文章。

鮑端磊（Daniel J. Bauer）

美國威斯康辛大學比較文學博士。天主教神父，現為天主教輔仁大學英國語文學系副教授。近年來，英譯的中文短篇故事，散見於*The Chinese Pen*、*The Free China Review*及*Inter-religio*（香港）等期刊。譯有《跟李伯伯學英文》一書。自一九九五年九月以來，即每星期為英文《中國郵報》（*The China Post*）撰寫專欄，討論有關教育及社會議題。目前在輔仁大學英國語文學系所開設的課程有翻譯、十八世紀英國文學、二十世紀初美國文學等。

校訂者簡介

彭淮棟

一九五三年生，畢業於東海大學外文系、台大外文研究所。現為報社編譯。譯有薩依德《鄉關何處》、《論晚期風格：反常合道的音樂與文學》；以撒・柏林《現實意識》；安伯托・艾可《美的歷史》、《醜的歷史》等多部。

邱明瀚

國立台灣師範大學英語系學士，美國亞利桑那州立大學英語教學進修，現職為中學英語教師，並致力於英語教材編與翻譯。著有《實用短句【快讀筆記本】》、《基礎文法【快讀筆記本】》。

繪者簡介

潔子

和貓孩子們住在有山有海的小村莊。落雨時，聽雨聲；豔陽天，曬太陽。食無肉也食無魚，喜歡泥土味青草香，喜歡手執畫筆的鄉野之人。